DOUBLE SOLITAIRE

DOUBLE SOLITAIRE

a novel

CRAIG NOVA

ARCADE
CRIME WISE

An Arcade CrimeWise Book

First Arcade CrimeWise Edition

This is a work of fiction. Names, places, characters, and incidents are either the products of the author's imagination or are used fictitiously.

Arcade Publishing books may be purchased in bulk at special discounts for sales promotion, corporate gifts, fund-raising, or educational purposes. Special editions can also be created to specifications. For details, contact the Special Sales Department, Arcade Publishing, 307 West 36th Street, 11th Floor, New York, NY 10018 or arcade@skyhorsepublishing.com.

Arcade Publishing® and CrimeWise® are registered trademarks of Skyhorse Publishing, Inc.®, a Delaware corporation.

Visit our website at www.arcadepub.com.

10 9 8 7 6 5 4 3 2 1

Library of Congress Cataloging-in-Publication Data is available on file.

Cover design by Erin Seaward-Hiatt
Jacket photograph © Alexander Turnbough/EyeEm/Getty Images

ISBN: 978-1-950691-22-7
Ebook ISBN: 978-1-950691-23-4

Printed in the United States of America

He who fights too long against dragons becomes a dragon himself: and if thou gaze too long into the abyss, the abyss will gaze into thee.

—Friedrich Nietzsche

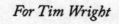

For Tim Wright

DOUBLE SOLITAIRE

1

FARRELL KNEW AFTER BEING IN Terry Peregrine's house for twenty minutes, that Terry was thinking about killing the girl from Alaska. Terry's anxious gestures, his handsome face, pale with worry and lack of sleep, his jumpy primping in front of a mirror, his obvious panic, all revealed his lack of control. The girl was sixteen, maybe younger, but she didn't look it. Her hair wasn't blond so much as silver, not white, and her eyes seemed purple, but Farrell, who had been sent to take care of this, thought, No, no. No one really has purple eyes. But there she was.

Peregrine's house was just off Mulholland on the north side of the hill that separated Los Angeles from the Valley. The house was a comfortable, stucco covered place in the Spanish style with those half pipe tiles on the roof and doors with wrought iron hinges. Three stories, a large backyard with eucalyptus trees growing at the back of the three-acre lot, trimmed to ensure privacy, but not enough to hide the view of the valley. A swimming pool in the backyard gave off the scent of chlorine, like an enormous, aquamarine flower. It was always shocking what the pool men knew, considering what they discovered on the bottom when the robot vacuum cleaner collected discarded items, condoms, bathing suit bottoms, needles, rubber tubes, and the like.

As an actor, Terry Peregrine was close to being completely virtual. He was good looking in a mildly unpleasant way, and while he had gotten a lot of attention, even to the extent to being what is known as a star, the falseness of how he came into being couldn't be avoided. He had been manufactured in the usual way, promoted, protected, and sold like a new deodorant. It happens all the time. Still, he had been cast in a high budget picture that was filming now. He was a hymn to falseness.

It was a September evening, and as Farrell had waited before knocking on Peregrine's door, the lights in the Valley reminded him of being a kid at the movies when he had eaten some candy called Jujubes, those chewy globes, like gummy bears, only smaller, and brightly colored, red, yellow, green, purple. The valley looked like it had been covered with them, from one end to the other, bright, mystical in random red, green, and yellow, and while the lights were packed together, they had a presence that only came out at night to reassure you, to make you think that things were really beautiful after all and benign. In the afternoon the Valley had an ominous clutter.

Farrell had knocked on the heavy wood of the door, the sound distant and throbbing like the last beating of a heart. Peregrine had opened the door with that look of someone cornered, his eyes moving from side to side, as though to see if anyone else was in his yard. The only other object was Farrell's gray Camry, which was as anonymous a car as he was able to find.

"Braumberg send you?" said Terry.

"Just tell me about it," said Farrell. "Can I come in?"

"If Braumberg sent you. Everything's going to be fine, right?" said Terry.

"How old is she?" said Farrell.

"She looks pretty old," he said.

"Uh-huh," Farrell said. "But that's not what I asked."

"Come on in, pal," he said. "We'll get this straight."

Pal, thought Farrell. You poor son of a bitch.

"You've got to u-u-understand," Farrell said.

Farrell's stutter came first with a sense of an interior jumpiness, and awareness of a presence, not quite a personality, but still having a will of its own that insisted on revealing items that Farrell wanted to keep hidden, anger, embarrassment, fury, frustration, and something else, an exasperation he couldn't ever name but which existed as a constant companion and an unnamed yearning, love, loneliness, mystification.

Terry waited for a moment, unsure about the stutter.

"It doesn't happen very often," Farrell said.

"All right," said Terry. "She's inside."

"Let's take a look," Farrell said.

If Farrell swallowed he could stop the stutter, but he had to do it at a precise moment. This morning Farrell had worked on it, and had said in his kitchen, "beggar," "hacksaw," "shadow," and "vanish."

"So things are b-b-better," said Terry. He smiled. "Now that you're here."

"How old . . ." Farrell swallowed.

"I told you what she looks like," said Terry.

The living room was cold, with AC blasting, white sofas curved around a glass table. It was impossible to say how many lines of chopped drugs had been laid out there, and then vacuumed through straws or rolled up bills, slightly moist from being passed from person to person as they sat there at night. They sniffed and looked at that red, yellow, and green glitter in the valley.

The curtains were pulled back. In the distance the San Gabriel Mountains were invisible aside from the streetlamps, which appeared like white Christmas lights thrown over a black whale. More and more, the houses in the mountains there were burning to the ground, since they were built in places where the eucalyptus trees still grew. Even though the people who owned the houses tried to keep the brush back, when a fire started it was time to get the hell out of the way.

Peregrine's hands were shaking, but it was hard to tell if this was from a hard comedown or the realization of what he was up against. He was short, as many actors are, since they are easier to photograph when they aren't very tall. Brownish hair, blue eyes, a nice smile, and he spent enough time in the gym to look fit.

The girl from Alaska sat on the sofa, dressed in her blue jeans, a tight-fitting sweater, some Adidas running shoes. Farrell guessed she was a little scared but not as much as she should have been. She turned toward him, the light in the room making that silver-blond hair seem all the more metallic. Her skin was as white as the keys of a new piano. Everything about her, the way she sat with that precise posture, her steady gaze, her beautiful skin, her breathy voice, even the perfume she wore, which while cheap, was changed by her presence, suggested a frank innocence perfectly blended with some ache, some desire. She didn't have a clue, thought Farrell. Not a clue.

He sat down.

"So, you're from Alaska," said Farrell.

"Have you ever been there?" she said.

"No," Farrell. "I hear the fishing is good."

"Shitload of salmon," she said. "If I never eat another piece of salmon it will be too soon. I worked in a cannery. You know what the sound is? Bang! Bang! Yeah, I'm from Alaska."

"What's your name?" said Farrell.

She stared right at him.

"Mary Jones," she said. "Will that do it?"

"That's funny," said Farrell. "My name is Jones, too."

"Maybe we're related," she said.

"Could be," said Farrell.

"Are you the one that's got the money?" she said.

"Maybe I can get it," said Farrell.

"I don't want any trouble," she said. She gestured to Terry. "He should know better than having anything to do with a girl my age. You know that, don't you, Terry?"

"You look older," said Terry.

"I get it. You can tell that to the police. They'll understand. Yeah, they'll say. You got confused. Sure."

"Terry gets confused easily," said Farrell.

"Hey," said Terry. "Don't, you know, condescend . . ."

"Look," said the girl from Alaska. "I just want to go home. This is no town for a kid from a small town in a place like Alaska. You know that?"

"Yes," said Farrell. "As a matter of fact, I do."

"You wouldn't believe what the winters are like," said the girl. "You don't know what cold is . . ."

The most important thing, thought Farrell, is to make sure she leaves with me.

"I know a girl who dropped the keys to her car in the middle of winter. She lived in Point Hope. You know, she took off her gloves to pick them up, and she lost a couple of fingers to frostbite."

"That's cold," said Farrell.

"Not as cold as this place," said the girl. "It's a different kind but it's even worse. You can lose all kinds of things to it."

"How much do you want?" said Farrell.

"I really want to go home," she said.

Farrell leaned closer. She had a lovely quality, really, and he liked her, even though she was threatening. It had been a long time since he had seen such innocence, such straightforward honesty, although that innocence made it impossible for the girl to understand her present circumstances.

Farrell glanced at Terry, who picked at his hands, then his face, then looked out the window.

"You've got an early call," said Farrell. "That's what Braumberg says. You're right in the middle of it, right. How many shooting days?"

"Sixty," said Terry. "We've done half. It's gonna be big. The Chinese box office is terrific these days. They love car crashes and we have car crashes up the kazoo . . ."

"Who's Braumberg?" said Mary Jones.

"A guy who finances pictures," said Terry.

"You mean like a producer," she said.

"Yes," said Farrell.

"You know, at one time I would have been interested in meeting a guy like that. Not now. I just want to go home."

"Sure," said Farrell.

"The winters are so clean. And cold. I want to be where you can spit and it freezes before it hits the ground. A diamond colored drop. Where the bears are dangerous. It's better than . . ." She gestured to the valley. "That."

"How much?" said Farrell.

She turned her eyes on him, the look in them one of longing for the north, for those long stretches of the Alcan highway. Farrell wondered if she had hitchhiked from Anchorage to LA. If any girl of her age could do it, she was the one. The more Farrell sat there, the more he liked her.

"Twenty thousand," she said. "Cash. No checks or anything that can be stopped. You can go right to an ATM."

"Terry?" said Farrell.

"I'm not paying that," he said. "If anyone has to pay it's going to be Braumberg. You know how much he has invested in this thing?"

Farrell stared at him for a while, then looked at Mary Jones.

"I don't want any trouble," said Mary Jones. "I don't want publicity, cops, or anything like that. I just want to go home. But if you think you can push me around, you are wrong. Just give me my money and I will go."

"Terry?" said Farrell.

"No, no, no," said Terry. "Who the fuck does this little . . ."

"Don't say it," said Farrell.

"You don't get it," said Mary Jones. "He can call me anything he wants. I don't care. I want my money and I want to go home."

"She isn't getting it from me," said Terry. "Not with the risk to Braumberg."

"I'll have to talk to him," said Farrell.

"You do that," said Terry.

"Yes," said Mary Jones. "Isn't that what you do? Don't you take care of things like this?"

"Sometimes," he said.

She nodded. Yeah, sure.

The scent of eucalyptus from the hillside, the earthy whiff of the fall in California, the medicinal odor of the chlorine in the swimming pool left that mood of LA, hope so perfectly mixed with the possibilities of disaster. It was in the air, as though the atmosphere was pressured, too, like a fault in the earth that extended above ground. Mary Jones sat there, as unmovable as a fireplug.

"So, from one Jones to another," said Mary Jones. "Talk to who you have to talk to."

"All right," said Farrell.

"That other guy was utterly worthless," said Mary Jones.

"What other guy?" said Farrell.

"No one, no one," said Terry, waving his hand, as though a mosquito was hovering around him. "She's so screwy. She doesn't know if she's on Zork or not."

"I know right where I am," said Mary Jones.

"Where are you staying?" said Farrell.

"I've got a motel on Ventura," said Mary Jones. "There's bugs in it. A lizard was in my room."

"Have you got a handbag?" said Farrell. "Any clothes?"

She gestured to a chair on by the large, fieldstone fireplace. The jacket was white, imitation leather, the kind of thing that probably looked elegant in Anchorage.

"I think you should come with me," said Farrell.

"Not on your life," she said.

"I think you should come with me," said Farrell.

She shook her head.

"Try to get me to leave," she said. "I dare you."

"You dare me?" said Farrell.

He liked her even more. Then he shook his head. If she only knew. Youth can't imagine what is behind the appearance of things.

"I still think you should come with me," he said.

"No," she said. "If I go with you, and you dump me in my motel, I won't have a chance. I want to call the cops, if I have to, from right here. No. I'm not going anywhere. Talk to the guy with money."

"Terry?" Farrell said. "Have you got the cash?"

"I'm not paying," said Terry.

Farrell stood by the fieldstone of the fire place, the little flecks of bright pyrite giving him the illusion that he was seeing pieces of light, like bits of the tail of a shooting star. The scent of the hillside had, in the way only this landscape could do, a hint of the morning fog, a little salty, as though a malign perfume was lingering. He said to Mary Jones, "I think you should c-c-come with me."

She shook her head.

"Twenty thousand dollars and I go home. I will just disappear."

"I'll talk to him, to Braumberg, first thing in the morning."

Outside Farrell sat in his car, that anonymous, gray Camry, the lights in the Valley shimmering in the distance. He glanced at the house, which had the lights on downstairs, but above that it was dark, a silhouette, as though cut from black cardboard against the Valley. He was surprised how much he admired Mary Jones's spunk, or that quality that only came from those long winters in Alaska. He had the momentary impulse to drive her back here. Still, he couldn't get that kind of money out of an ATM, didn't have it at home, and so it would have to be tomorrow. He still didn't like it.

The stutter showed itself like a little man, or a presence that Farrell saw as an advisory, but yet it helped him, too, since when he had trouble speaking, he saw how people reacted. That told him a lot.

"Mary Jones," he said. He shook his head. "Spitting like a diamond."

2

"YOU'RE LATE," SAID BRAUMBERG at eight in the morning. "Did you see the girl and Terry?"

"Sort of," Farrell said.

Braumberg sat on the wall around the Hollywood Bowl fountain. It had a large pool, about twenty feet across, and when Farrell had been at Hollywood High, he and some friends had tried to put enough detergent in the pool to make, as they had hoped, a five-foot wall of suds move across Highland. Still, it hadn't worked. The problem had been low sudsing soap. Farrell considered how reassuring it was to think of the soap, or the pranks pulled when he had been young. The soap had been in the same league as when Farrell and some friends tried to put enough gelatin in a swimming pool to make it into a large, chlorine scented, blue piece of Jell-O. The notion had been that a swimmer would dive in, only to bounce a couple of times. Farrell considered Mary Jones and what pranks she had pulled in Anchorage beyond freezing spit. Throwing a bucket of water on the sidewalk in January? Farrell felt the ghost of the pleasure he had taken in such youthful stunts, a sort of quick high, and he wondered, too, if the stunts had been training for the real trouble adults faced.

The bench at the fountain was a good, private place. The temple of the Vedanta Society on a hill opposite the Bowl seemed out of place, but that was true for many things, although the temple still produced a tug, a slight gravity. The traffic on Highland had a serpentine movement, a starting and stopping like a snake slithering toward the kill. The cars were a perfect mixture of the ridiculously expensive and clunkers, Ferraris alongside old Pintos rusted into red lace. The odd thing is that the drivers of each were equally angry.

"Yeah?" said Braumberg. "I'm all ears."

"I don't know," Farrell said. He swallowed just in time.

"Just what don't you know?" he said. "A lot of money is involved here. More than before. A lot more than before. So you think you understand, but you don't," Braumberg said. Then he stared at that traffic. Over Highland, a long cloud of smoke hung, which looked like an enormous yellow boa that stretched from the freeway down to the place where Highland turned to the east a little before it came to Hollywood Boulevard. The drivers in the cars were all wearing ear buds, all twitching differently to what they heard.

Maybe, Farrell thought, as he looked across Highland at the temple of the Vedanta Society. He could check into their retreat in Santa Barbara for a month. No talking.

"What do you think?" said Braumberg.

"I think Terry is hiding in his own asshole," said Farrell. "He is thinking about killing that girl."

"What did you say?"

"What did I say?" said Farrell.

He shook his head.

"I tried to get her out of there," said Farrell.

"And?" said Braumberg.

"She's smart enough to know that staying right there gives her credibility."

"So, she wouldn't leave?"

"That's right," said Farrell.

"Then take care of it," said Braumberg. "That's your job."

Braumberg wanted to look anonymous when he met Farrell and so he wore new jeans, a work shirt, Wolverine boots, and had a red bandana sticking out of his rear pocket. This was Braumberg's idea of what a carpenter looked like, but it wouldn't fool anyone.

Still, Braumberg had the California Disease, just like everyone else. Or, maybe he had the condition more than others. Maybe this explained why Braumberg was getting more generous with the money he gave Farrell to fix something, although Farrell had to admit the problems were getting worse, too. Part of the California Disease was the belief that you could buy your way out of fraud. Braumberg surely believed this. After all, in California there wasn't much you couldn't get with cash.

The Disease was the notion that you could invent yourself out of nothing, or out of TV advertisements, movie roles, posters, songs, country and western or punk styles, or any style, and that all you needed was a certain mood and a hint of mystery.

It took Farrell a while to tease out the details, but Braumberg had grown up in Brooklyn, attended City College, and then came west, pretended he had gone to Harvard, although he was cagey about it, never saying so out right, just hinting around about having been in Porcellian. And, of course, he was cagey enough to refer to it as the Porc. The only better thing in Hollywood would have been Oxford, but Braumberg was smart enough to know that while he could pull off an accent that was Brooklyn by way of Harvard, he wasn't adept enough to do so for Brooklyn by way of Trinity College, Oxford. The first time Farrell had met Braumberg to help with an actor's trouble, Farrell was pretty sure Braumberg wasn't what he seemed (a good bet in LA with just about everyone). Still,

Braumberg gave money to some charities, although always careful not to give too much. He was now right where he wanted to be as a producer, at least socially, that is, he was legitimate but mysterious ... which, in Los Angeles, meant he was "legit" but shy about some things that people could only imagine. And, of course, people did imagine things: an affair with a woman who was a French aristocrat, an illegitimate child by a beautiful woman in Buenos Aires. Really, the sky was the limit.

"You look like you are getting windy," Braumberg said.

"No," said Farrell.

"So, what are we going to do?" said Braumberg.

"Pay her," said Farrell. "It's too bad she wouldn't let me drive her to the motel where she is staying."

"And you think she will go away?" said Braumberg.

"There's only one way to find out," said Farrell.

The odor of Braumberg's new jeans mixed with the fish pond scent of the fountain.

Braumberg, in spite of everything, was a religious man, and Farrell supposed in moments like this religion gave him comfort. It was one of the reasons Farrell really liked him. Neither one of the two men had ever planned on ending up at moments like these, and this surprise made them more empathetic with each other.

"You shouldn't have fixed Terry's mess the way you did last time," Farrell. "You guaranteed that there would be more trouble, and, this is it."

"I thought that giving a DNA sample to the cops would be a proof of innocence while I got the girl involved and her mother to take a slow boat to Australia ...."

Farrell swallowed and looked at the traffic.

"You shouldn't have done that," said Farrell.

"I thought he had learned his lesson," said Braumberg.

"Sure, sure," Farrell said. "That m-m-makes sense."

"You don't have to get snooty about it," said Braumberg. "What's gotten into you?"

Farrell thought about for a minute. What's gotten into me? He craved dignity more than anything else. But how could you be dignified in a town like this? And he liked the girl from Alaska. He really did.

"Did you ever read Kierkegaard?" Farrell said.

"Who's that? Sounds like a Danish director. Depressing movies about love gone wrong . . . or suicide pacts . . . or kids with cancer . . ."

"You didn't take philosophy at Harvard?"

Braumberg winced and said, "Come on, Farrell. Something is eating at you. You aren't your cheerful usual self."

"I don't know," Farrell said. "Kierkegaard said that the nature of despair is precisely not to know one is despairing."

"Maybe," said Braumberg. "I bet he still makes shitty movies. Didn't he make *Dark Love*? Those fucking Danes. And yet, you know, they have respectable box office. Or the Swedes do."

"I'll have to look at one of Kierkegaard's old movies again," Farrell said.

"All right," said Braumberg. "Enough film 101."

"Here's what we are going to do," said Farrell. "I'm going to go to the bank and get the money she wants. Then I'm going to give it to her and drive her to the airport. With any luck she will be back in Anchorage by tomorrow."

Braumberg sighed.

"Good. Good. You are one of the few people in this town I can trust."

"Trust," said Farrell. He winced, bit his lip. "Okay. I've to go to the bank."

"The bank," said Braumberg. "I've had it up to here with banks.

A lot of people got hurt in the mortgage slump," said Braumberg. "This town is all about mortgages, you know that?"

"It makes the place look better than it is," said Farrell.

"And we're just getting back to normal," said Braumberg.

"Normal," said Farrell. "Yeah, sure."

"You know what a tranche is?" said Braumberg.

"A piece of a security," said Farrell. "A lot depends on which piece you have."

"You're telling me?" said Braumberg. "A lot of people got hurt."

"You didn't lose your house, did you?" said Farrell.

"No," said Braumberg.

"So, you didn't get screwed too bad," said Farrell. "A lot of people lost a house."

"I thought things were going to get better," said Braumberg. "Those fucking banks. And now this. Peregrine and that girl from Alaska."

"I'll get the cash," said Farrell.

"I'll reimburse you, and, of course, give you your fee," said Braumberg.

The Bank of America branch was at Sunset and Vine, and the place looked like a combination of an aircraft carrier and an ancient temple. Flat roof, two stories, cheesy columns going up forty feet, a neon sign with the bank logo. The teller, a middle-aged woman with the skin of a serious smoker, what Farrell thought of as a cancer tan, took Farrell's check without blinking.

Farrell considered a business he was buying, Coin-A-Matic, which he thought could explain why so much cash was flowing through his account without any reason. The closing was coming up, and Farrell could already feel the slight change that would take place in him, just by owning a vending machine company. Not quite the effect of a magic wand, but something nevertheless.

"Hundreds?"

"Please," said Farrell.

The woman pushed the envelopes with the bank's logo on them across the counter, which was imitation marble, and Farrell put them in the pocket of his Patagonia vest. He looked like he worked in the front office for Outward Bound. Even these clothes left him aware of some attitude that made him speak in a slightly different way.

"Thanks," said Farrell.

"Don't spend it all in one place," said the teller.

"That's good advice," said Farrell.

"Doesn't look like you are going to take it," said the teller.

"No," said Farrell. "I'm afraid not."

Farrell's house was in Laurel Canyon, on a side street that came off the main road about halfway between Sunset and Mulholland. The house looked like it had been moved from the coast of Maine. It was a story and a half, a cape with a pitched roof, and its shingles were the color of fog. At the front door an arbor had been build and roses grew on it. Glowing Dawn was the variety, and they were in their last bloom of the fall.

Upstairs, Farrell's house had a bedroom, a bath, and a library. The library was an extravagance, but it was where he spent his evenings, when he read Tacitus, Xenophon, Herodotus, and, yes, even Kierkegaard. He had a complete *Oxford English Dictionary*, not the one that required reading with a magnifying glass, but twenty volumes. Using an online dictionary, as far as Farrell was concerned, was like taking a bath with his socks on. He didn't want anyone to know, given his job, that he was bookish, and he reassured himself by asking how many bookish men have a Sig Sauer pistol, a P320 semiautomatic, in a drawer next to the book shelves. When he picked it up, out of the drawer, it had a valence that made him careful and then, for a while, the scent of Hoppe's oil clung to his hand. Downstairs, the fireplace had a gas pipe with perforations to light eucalyptus logs, which were stacked in the backyard. On the wall of his kitchen, opposite the table where he ate alone, he had a framed map of the Paris Métro. The shapes of the lines were angular, but the colors of them were as bright and cheerful as tulips, daffodils, and the blue lines were the color of delphiniums. Between jobs, when Farrell had a week or a month or even more time, he went to Paris, which was as far away from Los Angeles as you could get. He often stared at the map for stops he used, Odeon, Rue du Bac, or Saint-Michel. He had a tutor there, a French woman who intimidated him, but he learned a little of the language, which was another way of escaping Los Angeles. No one would ever say in Hollywood, *Je suis désolé*. I'm sorry.

Farrell's solitary life had slowly become part of him, like a substance he had absorbed, but he accepted it as necessary, since most of what he did required discretion or outright silence, and in the past, sooner or later, a girlfriend would say, "Well, when are you going to tell me what you do?"

So, he lived alone, cooked on his three-thousand-dollar culinary stove, read at night, and tried to be discreet.

He avoided looking in the mirror. When he did, he felt the delicate sense of being in the presence of two people, the man in the glass and the interior sense of someone opposite the image. He had a bench and weights, and he stayed in shape, not so much as to look like a Navy SEAL, but enough to be able to take someone's arm so that they knew he meant it. About five feet, eleven inches. Grayish hair, not from age, that was a sheet metal color, cut short. A scar in a left brow from someone's right hand. Nose that hinted at a bird of prey. Greenish eyes, the color of money. He looked away, relieved to have that physical presence of another version of himself fall away like a sheet over a statue that is being unveiled. A cool relief to be alone again, without the emotional static.

About a hundred feet away another house had been built. It was a lot like Farrell's although it was a little bigger, still covered with those weathered shingles, but it didn't have roses around the door. The house next door had been vacant for about two months, and the emptiness had left to Farrell in a mood that was like waiting for some unknown but compelling event. Both houses were behind a privet hedge that went along the road.

He sat at the table in the kitchen with the envelopes from the bank filled with hundred-dollar bills, which, just by their weight, left Farrell considering how anonymous cash was and how oddly powerful. He took out his phone, scrolled down to Terry's number, and when he was about to touch the call button the phone rang. Terry Peregrine.

"I was just going to call you," said Farrell.

"Yeah, yeah," said Terry. "But it's all set."

"Is that right?" said Farrell.

"It's all set," said Terry. "She came to her senses. I gave her five thousand bucks and left her at the bus station."

"No kidding?" said Farrell.

"Yeah," said Terry. "She's a smart kid. Just wanted to go home."

"H-h-home," said Farrell.

"Yeah. No problem. You can tell Braumberg to relax. All of this is a nonproblem problem."

Farrell let the silence between them linger, a sort of dark static.

"She said she was going to send a postcard when she got home," said Terry. "You know, a picture of the mountains or a bear."

"You better let me see it," said Farrell.

"What's the big deal?" said Terry.

"I'm going to want to see the card," said Farrell.

"Don't give it a second thought," said Terry. "Nothing to worry about."

"I'm going to be waiting," said Farrell.

"Calm down," said Terry. "I'll let you know. Sometime."

"Not sometime," said Farrell.

"Okay," said Terry. "I'll take care of it."

Farrell put the phone on the table.

That card better come, thought Farrell.

He sat at the breakfast table and looked at the hillside behind his house, but he kept seeing the odd, metallic colored hair and those peculiar eyes of Mary Jones. She was right about it being cold here, although it was of a different kind than in Alaska. There were things Farrell did and things he wouldn't do. When he got an idea, he stuck with it. His friends, when he had had friends, called him Mad Dog, and now, when he sat there, he thought it was apt.

He was alert to a slight tremor, which for a moment he thought was the beginning of an earthquake, a mild, almost impossible to apprehend shaking. And yet, it left him with a suspicion of something else, which was the item that had gotten him into trouble and that had caused him to make mistakes. And why should it occur now, like an almost impossible to perceive shaking of the ground? Anger, he thought. That's anger. I've got to keep it under control, to get a better grip. Not let it emerge out of the shadows. And yet the temptation, almost sensual, to let it out was right there and a reason for him to be more concerned than ever.

Mad Dog had been only one of the things he had been called. He didn't mind this one so much, but some others had changed him. Or the word was an entrance to something so deep he only knew a door was opening when he heard it. Farrell's father, now dead, had been an engineer at Lockheed Martin Skunk Works. His orderly, engineer way of thinking and of doing things, from parallel parking to balancing a checkbook, had made it difficult for him to warm up to Farrell's late hours, defiance, or Farrell's natural anger at being disliked because he wasn't obviously on his way to engineering school.

Farrell had left home at seventeen to move in with the family of a friend. The word that had finished whatever slender connection there had been between Farrell and his father had been used in the last argument. His father, who struggled with being inarticulate and unable to speak easily, aside from engineering jargon, had said, "You are nothing but a bum. A bum. You hear me?"

The word was a summation of every devastating notion his father felt about Farrell and wanted to say, but couldn't.

The last thing Farrell had said, over his shoulder when he went out the door, was, "Don't say that. Don't. I'm not a bum."

Still, even now, in the hum of the refrigerator, he detected a slight, infuriating memory of the word. It wasn't something anyone should say to him. Ever. The accusation left him with a fury that he kept tucked away. Or tried to. It infuriated him not because of the word, or the notion of being a man with a bottle of wine in a bag, but because it had been used as a complete indictment of him from someone who couldn't understand.

3

IF SHE WENT BY BUS, that's probably a couple of days, thought Farrell, and then it would take a while to go home to her parents' house, if she spent any time with them, but after that she'd need time to find a place of her own and to get a job. Say, two weeks, and then there was the mail, which would probably take a week. Two to three weeks, Farrell thought.

Farrell's accountant, Myron Lee, was an obese man with full cheeks like a hamster, shiny skin, and who wore rayon shirts that seemed to put off a variety of financial stink. Myron called to say that the closing for the vending machine company was all set.

In the afternoon, before rush hour, which was the hottest part of the day even in September, a woman in a small U-Haul truck, with its orange and silver stripes, like the American flag of transience, drove through the break in the privet hedge. Farrell's window had a view of the drive that branched to his house and then to the house next door. He stood at his window, counting the days before that card would come.

The woman's posture, her hands on the wheel of the truck and the ease with which she drove, made him hesitate. The movement seemed to be competence personified.

The list of the morning's words was on the counter, printed from a website for people with a stutter. The little man, or whatever it was that caused trouble, seemed to wake up.

Hubcap, humbug, lemon . . . tight fit . . .

"Humbug," he said.

She got out of the small truck with the orange advertisements on the sides, and put her hands on the hips of her tight-fitting blue jeans as she faced her house. The woman had a glow, since her skin took the light with a perfect absorption. Like pale makeup. She wore a T-shirt that said over her chest, CHILDREN'S HOSPITAL, UCLA. She had light brown hair, in a chignon, freckles across her nose, and the posture of a dancer.

Her shoulders were square, and her jeans fit perfectly. She turned one way, as though limbering up, and finally walked toward Farrell's house, her lips in the morning light the color of perfectly ripe raspberries.

Farrell considered that he saw new people all the time, and so why should a particular one make the light seem brighter, or the colors more distinct, or leave that odd sensation which, with just a little encouragement, turns into a subtle vibration, almost neural, not trembling but with a little encouragement could be.

She put her face, with that spray of freckles across her nose, to the window of Farrell's kitchen, and then she tapped on the glass with the neatly trimmed nail of her index finger.

He pointed at himself and mouthed, "Me?"

She mouthed, "Yes. You."

The door opened with a hush.

She stood in the roses, which now at the end of the season still resisted those cold mornings, and the fragrance of them was like paradise. She breathed deeply, kept her eyes on him. He couldn't tell if it was the scent of the roses or her skin, in that heat of the day, that seemed to linger. She had a small mustache of sweat on her upper lip.

"Hi," she said. "I'm your new neighbor. Rose Marie."

She put out her hand. Her palm had a warmth and a caressing effect that was out of all proportion to a neighbor introducing herself. He thought, You are too alone to even notice this. This is not for you.

After she let go, he realized he had already taken some infinitely small thing, just in the touch. She trembled, too. He was sure of it. A moral quality showed in her movement, in her smile, in her ease with herself, although it was perfectly imbued, too, with a sultry instinct. Maybe the moral quality had something to do with that T-shirt with the Children's Hospital logo.

"Quinn Farrell," he said. "Everyone calls me Farrell."

She sighed.

"Don't these roses smell wonderful," she said.

"I always think it's like paradise," he said.

She looked at him, considering. He winced.

"I mean, like a good place . . ." he said.

"Paradise," she said. "It's nice to think so, isn't it?" She swallowed. "What do you think it's like?"

"Paradise?" he said. "Well, I don't know. I've never been, but I've come close a couple of times."

"You mean someone almost killed you?" she said.

"Well, you know," he said. "It's LA. A lot of people around here have crazy ideas."

She went on looking at him.

Then she took another deep breath and said, "Well, are you going to help me with my things in the truck? I had someone lined up, but, well, you know . . ."

"I've got a business appointment . . ." he said.

"Oh," she said.

"But you know what? It will keep . . ." he said.

"You don't look like someone who's late very often," she said.

She kept her eyes on him and gave him a two-hundred-watt smile.

"I don't know. There's always a first time," he said.

"The first time?"

That smile again.

"Was it a boyfriend who was supposed to help you?" Farrell said.

More of that smile.

"Wouldn't you like to know . . . ?" she said.

"Okay," Farrell said. "I'll give you a hand."

"Good," she said. "Yeah. It was a boyfriend. Or someone I used to live with . . . He may come around sometime . . ."

"I didn't mean to p-p-pry," Farrell said.

"Tell me another," she said.

How polite, how considerate, he thought, that she ignores the stutter.

Rose Marie's movement had a sense of a cool cleanliness or an impossible to describe grace. It reminded Farrell of a swan he had seen at the edge of a lake, its locomotion seeming to take place without effort.

Farrell said, "I'll give you a hand."

"Are you good with three-dimensional things? I've got a sofa I don't think is going to go through the door."

"You know what the trick is? You turn it on its side so it goes through the door like an L."

He swallowed.

"It's a . . . tight fit," he said.

"Yeah. It is a tight fit," she said.

"Tight fit," he said.

When they bumped into each other, with the sofa, chairs, a table, and rugs, it was the most natural thing in the world, and when she reached around a corner to find his hand, her scent, like a fresh pond, was right there. That small line of moisture along her hairline and on her upper lip was gin colored. She smiled and wiped her brow.

"Hot, isn't it?" she said. "You know, I thought you were going to sit there in your kitchen while I struggled with this." She gestured at her things in the living room, the brown boxes with brown, shiny tape, the sofa, and a leather chair. "But I'll be damned. You're a gentleman."

"I wouldn't go that far," Farrell said.

"Modest, too," she said. "All I ever meet in this town are vain assholes."

The freckles across her nose reminded him of an innocence, and how long had it been since he had felt something like innocence? No, not innocence. Something really dangerous. A moral presence. Dignity. He stood there with an ache.

"Something wrong?" she said.

"No, no," he said. "I don't think there's anything wrong."

"It's been a long time since I've seen a gentleman," she said.

"Are you flirting with me?" Farrell said.

"No," she said. "Not really. Just a little fun."

"Okay. Sure," he said.

"You can figure it out," she said.

He moved a rug, a chair that had been made for comfortable reading, a brass light to go with it, the metal shade a little tarnished but all the more domestic for that, and some boxes of books. The top opened and there was *The Peloponnesian War*, *Tacitus*, *The War with Hannibal*, and *The March Up Country*.

Uh-oh, he thought. Real trouble.

"There's a great moment in *The War with Hannibal*," he said. "About the town that goes over to the Carthaginians."

"The town cuts a deal with Hannibal," she said, "when it looks like he is going to win. Then the Roman's show up."

"Yeah," Farrell said. "That's it."

"Some mistakes are forever," she said.

He nodded, yes, yes, yes. That's all he had. A history of other people's mistakes.

"You remember what happened to the town?" he said.

"Yeah," she said. "The men went out to fight the Romans. The women with their kids stood on the wall of the town, and when it was clear their men had lost, they threw their kids over the wall and jumped."

"Well, I would have done the same. Given what the Romans had in mind . . ." he said.

"So the lesson is you want to be careful who you get involved with, right?"

Yes, he thought. He considered Mary Jones. Was she on the bus? That should have been a warning, that Terry put her on the bus, but maybe someone like Mary Jones would like the bus.

Farrell gestured to the logo on her shirt.

"What's that?"

"The Children's Hospital?" she said. "It's where I work."

"What do you do?"

"Me? Oh, it's hard to say exactly."

She turned her grayish eyes on him. How had she managed to get her hooks into him, just by moving a sofa, some cardboard boxes, a rug, and a box of kitchen utensils?

His Camry sat in the circular drive that went by his front door. She took it in, just like that, and said, "If I judged by what kind of car you drove, I'd say you were a cop. You can't get more anonymous than a gray Camry."

"What do you drive when it isn't a U-Haul truck?"

"A Subaru Legacy," she said.

"Same thing," he said.

"I have it because I'm too busy to really care," she said. "But I think you have yours for a reason."

Bingo. Shit. "I guess you could say that. Cars, people make such a big deal out of them."

They sat on her sofa in the middle of her living room, close together, not uneasy.

"All I can give you is a glass of water," she said. "But I'm not sure where the glasses are."

"It's okay," he said. "I told you about the meeting. Business."

"Thanks," she said.

"Sure," he said. "What are neighbors for?"

When he was at the door, able to feel her presence on his back, she said, "There's one last thing. Come over to the truck."

"What's that?" he said.

"A lot of people get freaked out," she said.

He raised a brow.

"You don't look like that kind," she said. "Here's the last thing."

The habitat, which sat on the bench seat of the U-Haul, was a large fish tank. Inside, like a pile of patched inner tubes, sat a Burmese python, and even though it was coiled, it was probably about ten feet long, thick in the middle.

"How much does it weigh?" said Farrell.

"About thirty-five pounds," she said. "Before eating."

"Arrogant?" he said. "Like, 'Where's my rat? You're late.'"

"Well, condescending. It helps if two people move it. The snake slides from side to side if you tip the tank."

The python moved a little when they opened the door of the U-Haul, and its locomotion had a fluid quality, like oil. Its eyes were tinted green, as though the cold oil of the creature's essence was colored with antifreeze, as a way of allowing for its existence, since it seemed cold, not so much to the touch as in attitude. Well, he thought, who would have thought she'd have a thing like that?

"So," said Rose Marie. "There it is. I guess you want some explanation."

"So long as it doesn't get out of this tank and come over to my house."

"It gets out," she said. "Come on. Help me carry it upstairs. There's an extra bedroom where we can put it."

"You don't look like the python type," he said.

"Is there a python type?" she said.

"You know, guys with glasses like coke bottles. Women with tattooed arms and a nose piercing."

That smile again.

"You haven't got a tattoo, do you?"

"Give a girl a little mystery," she said. "No, it's this way. The ex-boyfriend had it. You know, he was always disappearing and forgetting about it. He's an anthropologist, and he picked up just like that one time and went to India. Which wouldn't have been so bad for a month, but when he was there, in India, he took off his clothes and walked into a band of macaque monkeys. He spent a year with them. He knows more about monkeys than anyone on earth. What I got left with was Scooter."

"Scooter?"

"That's the python's name. And what was I going to do with it? Kill it? Let it go? You think that's a good idea . . . ?"

"You could ask people in Florida," he said.

"That's just what I mean," she said. "I don't know if it could live off of Mulholland Drive, in the brush, but I don't think we should find out, either. I could sell it, but then someone might let it go anyway, when they got tired of it. So, I'm stuck with it. A rat twice a month. Come on. Give me a hand."

They lifted the aquarium, carried it upstairs, the snake sliding one way and then another as the glass box was tilted on the stairs. They left it in a bedroom on the floor.

"The boyfriend was always vain about the way he dressed, but after spending time with the monkeys he was worse. The monkeys judged each other by the way they looked. He started thinking that way, too."

"So, the boyfriend is back now? Around here?"

She just looked at him.

"Yeah. Maybe he will come around to get Scooter."

"Don't people get frightened when they see it for the first time?" he said.

"Sometimes. But this is LA. What don't people see here?"

"LA," he said. He shook his head.

"You want to watch when I feed it?" she said.

"That's all right," he said. "I think I've got the idea."

"You don't know what you're missing," she said. With an effect like having a bottle of perfume waved under his nose, she winked.

"Since you don't mind me p-p-rying," he said.

"I didn't say that," said Rose Marie.

"I'll take a chance then," he said. "What went wrong?"

"With the ex-boyfriend?" she said.

She spent a moment, her eyes on the python, as though its sluggish coils were evidence of things she thought she had forgotten, and then, with surprising candor, she willingly told Farrell that the ex-boyfriend had been so charming as make you want to take off your shoes, but without warning he morphed into a man so angry that they had to pay a carpenter to fix the holes he made in the walls.

"So I couldn't take the . . ." she said.

"The fury," he said.

"Yeah," she said. "That right. The fury."

She spoke as though the word was a thing, an object she could hold in her hand, like a piece of pipe. She leaned close, bringing that scent of skin and hair, and said, "Thanks for the help."

"Sure," he said. "Any time. Just let me know when it gets out."

She smiled and said, "Okay."

He walked back to his house, but on the way he checked the car. He kept an extra set of keys, in a black magnetic box, attached to the bumper of the Camry, and when he came out of the house, on most days, he put his hand there, just to reassure himself the box was still there, although when he did, he felt the residue, the oil and grease that collected on it, as though the soul of Los Angeles was somehow perfectly melded with the exhaust on the freeways. The grease on the key box almost reassured him, since it seemed to be a confirmation of everything he knew about the city.

He wondered what picture would be on the postcard. A grizzly? Mountains with snow on them the color of a bride's dress? The card better come, thought Farrell. He didn't forget things and he wasn't going to forget this. Two to three weeks. That would be twenty more shooting days.

4

IT DIDN'T TAKE LONG FOR Nikolay and Pavel, two ex KGB employees, or whatever was used now in Moscow, to appear after the closing for Coin-A-Matic. Farrell guessed that the previous owner of Coin-A-Matic hadn't told the truth about them, but then who would tell a prospect buyer that a shakedown of three hundred dollars a month for protection was part of its normal business expenses. So, that's what you get, thought Farrell, for trying to appear legitimate. He should have known by his accountant's voice when the accountant had said, "You want to do this? Own this outfit? I don't advise it."

"I'll take a chance," said Farrell.

"Sign here," said the accountant.

Farrell wondered if the accountant, Myron Lee, took his short-sleeve rayon shirt home and washed it every other day, or if he had a collection of shirts that always seemed to be on their second day. Myron twitched when he spoke, a heft of one shoulder, as though what he was thinking gave him a little shock. He blinked and told a joke when he was uneasy, as though a laugh helped.

Farrell signed. Myron Lee said, "Well, you can't say I didn't warn you."

"We'll see," said Farrell.

"Sometimes you don't want to see," said Myron.

Myron twitched. Tucked his chin down so his wattle quivered.

"There were two lawyers who had just won a big case. They went to the beach."

"And?" said Farrell as he put his copy of the signed agreement in his jacket pocket.

"So, they are on the beach and see two figures in the distance. They get closer. The lawyers see it's two women. They don't have any clothes on. One lawyer says to the other, 'Maybe we can screw them.' The other lawyer says. 'For what?'"

Farrell's laugh was sincere, but a little bleak.

"Good luck," said the accountant. "I'll be here to do the books."

The building for Coin-A-Matic had been built for small manufacturing, made of cinder blocks with a double door in front so trucks or vans could go in and out. It used to house something called Movie Air, which made large fans that made a breeze for a movie set, or could be set up so an actor's hair would heave a little at the right moment. The fans had been about eight feet across, and the propellers inside looked as though they had come from an airplane, like a De Havilland Beaver. The building cost little to rent, since it was in the clutter belt south of Santa Monica Boulevard. Not dead yet as a neighborhood, but on life support. Just the way Farrell liked it. No one took anything too seriously in a place that was on the verge of becoming a slum.

Farrell had hired an old friend from Hollywood High to run the vending machine business day to day. Bob Marshall was in his thirties, and he had the limp of a man with a prosthetic leg. Marshall was short, heavy, and had been a child actor on a TV series called *San Pedro Blues*. He had lost a leg on a motorcycle a few years ago, and now he held up his socks with thumbtacks on his wooden leg. His childhood acting career was long gone, and he spent his time reading science fiction novels, which he bought by the pickup truck load, then, after reading them, sometimes two a day, he'd take the load back to a store on San Vicente, where he exchanged the books in his truck for half what he had paid, then loaded up his truck with a new supply.

After the closing, Farrell found the truck parked in front of the building where Coin-A-Matic had its office. Bob Marshall's back was to the street as he looked at some of the new titles in the bed of the truck.

"Hey, Bob," said Farrell. "Let's look around. It's all mine."

"Good, good," said Bob.

Bob dropped a yellowed book into the orderly piles of them in the bed of the truck.

"Still reading sci-fi," said Farrell.

"Couldn't live without it," said Marshall.

Farrell put the key into a small door that was set into a larger one at the front of the building.

"This place used to make fans," said Farrell. "For artificial wind."

Farrell opened the door. Inside some vending machines were along one wall, and along the other wall cases of Doritos, Oreos, cheese in orange crackers, bacon-flavored chips, all in small bags that went into the machines. A workbench was next to the machines, and above it were tools, wrenches, pliers, a set of Allen wrenches, ball-peen hammers and mallets, crescent wrenches, and an ohmmeter and other electronic devices to check the wiring of the machines. A laptop was on the workbench, and it plugged into the back of the newer machines to run diagnostic software. Sometimes a motherboard had to be replaced in a vending machine. Bob Marshall, after losing a leg, had spent a lot of time tinkering with machines, and he said he should be able to fix what went wrong. He said that this business, vending machines, was "all maintenance." Bob Marshall smiled when he said this and he said, too, that he "was just glad to have a job." It made him feel more real, he said.

The first week, Marshall drove the Coin-A-Matic van over the route, up the Cahuenga Pass out to Ventura and the Valley, which was, according to the previous owner, "A ghetto of vending machines." Marshall filled the machines, took the bills out of the sheet metal box where they fell after being put into the machines, and brought the money to the building south of Santa Monica Boulevard. "Just like hammering nails," he said. Farrell did the books. When he'd redeposited fifteen thousand of that twenty thousand dollars he hadn't given to Mary Jones, he'd also deposited the first haul from Coin-A-Matic. The woman with the cancer tan at the Bank of America took the cash without any curiosity, although she said, "If you've got a vending machine business, you should get a device to count money. Saves time."

"That's a good idea," said Farrell.

In the second week, in the evening, Farrell was at the office of Coin-A-Matic. Bob said one machine was "wonky," but he could fix it.

Nikolay and Pavel walked from their car, a black SUV, which they had parked across the street. Nikolay wore a tight T-shirt and looked as though he didn't realize the benefits from lifting weights were limited, and walked with a gait that wavered from side to side, not a swagger, but something that made Farrell look at him more directly. Pavel was heavyset, too, but more from pelmeni and vodka, heavy in the stomach, short legs, his face marked with acne scars. Nikolay was taller but seemed to be Pavel's older brother. Maybe it was just the expression, which reminded Farrell of the glance of a python. Not mean spirited, really, just all business. They had moved from Russia to Queens, and then from there to LA, where they thought it would be easier to make money.

Nikolay stepped through the small door in the large one at the front of the building.

"Let me introduce myself," said Nikolay.

"Yeah," said Pavel. He touched his gray skin and those scars that looked like a relief map of the moon. "We've got to talk."

"Oh, shit," said Farrell.

"That's right," said Nikolay.

"Who are these guys?" said Marshall.

"Who are we?" said Nikolay. "Let me explain."

It took about twenty minutes. They stood in the main room with the supplies for the vending machines, next to the bench with tools for repairing them, and it came down to three hundred dollars a month, "regular," said Pavel, and Farrell stood there, nodding, yes, yes, yes. Nikolay and Pavel already had a list of the places that had machines from Coin-A-Matic, and knew, too, which customers were difficult. For instance, there was a man from India who had a mini-mart on Ventura Boulevard, and he was flirting with signing with someone else. So, Nikolay said, "When an Indian in Studio City calls, you better treat him right."

"I noticed him," said Bob Marshall.

"That's good, my friend. That's very good," said Pavel.

"Word gets around," said Nikolay. "You know, if someone has a complaint. And, if someone has a complaint, then that means I have a complaint. Because if you lose business, then I lose business."

"Exactly," said Pavel.

Then Pavel and Nikolay went out the door with that swaying, vain gait, as though they had just had a large and very satisfying meal, and they left behind them an expensive scent that hung in the air like an invisible feather boa.

Marshall said, "Why did you go for this?"

Farrell opened the small door and stared at the two of them as they got into their black SUV.

"I can't have any trouble," said Farrell.

"Then why are you laughing," said Marshall.

Farrell went on, that deep, constant laugh echoing in the small warehouse. The boxes of chips, the cases of water and Coke and Red Bull that gave off the reassuring scent of cardboard.

"That laughing is making me uneasy," said Marshall.

"So," said Farrell. "I try to do the right thing. To pay taxes on what I make, and I get this? And you ask why I am laughing?"

"These guys don't look funny to me," said Marshall.

"No," said Farrell. "I guess not."

The van for Coin-A-Matic, which was parked near the front door, was new. Farrell looked at Marshall.

"You aren't having any trouble driving this?" said Farrell.

"No," said Marshall. "It's an automatic. No trouble."

"The route is okay? No problems?" said Farrell.

"Not until these two," said Marshall. He gestured toward the door.

Farrell put his hand to the side of one eye where the tears had collected.

"I wish you wouldn't laugh like that," said Marshall.

"If an Indian guy calls from Studio City," said Farrell. "Let's try to keep him happy."

"I can handle it," said Marshall. "That's not what I'm worried about."

"You can never tell," said Farrell.

Marshall pulled up his pant leg, took out the thumbtack that held up his sock, pulled the sock up, and put the thumbtack in. It had a red head, and the socks were blue.

"I think I'm going to go home," said Farrell.

"What are you going to do?" said Marshall.

"Read Thucydides," said Farrell. "Think things over."

"Like what?"

How much longer is it going to be until Terry Peregrine gets into more trouble? What Mary Jones is doing? When the card is going to come?

"T-t-his and that," said Farrell.

"Yeah, I know," said Marshall. "I got some good books in the bed of my truck. You know what? I've got a copy of *Tau Zero*."

"*Tau Zero*," said Farrell. "No kidding."

"A classic," said Marshall.

"So, stick with the route," said Farrell.

"No problem," said Marshall. "Piece of cake."

5

THREE WEEKS AFTER THE CLOSING for Coin-A-Matic, Braumberg called to say, "He's done it again. He says he may need your help."

"May? May?" said Farrell. "Can you tell me what that means, that 'may'?"

"I'll call you when I know," said Braumberg. "He didn't sound so good."

No kidding, thought Farrell.

"We haven't got too many shooting days left," said Braumberg.

"The problem will come later," said Farrell.

"We'll see," said Braumberg.

Yeah, thought Farrell, maybe the accountant is right. Sometimes it's better not to see.

In the weeks between the closing and the call about Terry having "done it again," Farrell had watched Rose Marie as she moved things around in her house, put up curtains, and loaded her car with cardboard boxes for the recycling center. She stopped by from time to time.

A few days before the call, Rose Marie tapped on his window, her freckles visible, a strand of hair in front of her nose, which she blew away, *poof*. . . . He opened the door and she stood there, looking him over.

"How's the unpacking going?" he said. "The moving in?"

"I just wanted to get away from . . ." she said. "The . . ."

"Clutter," he said. "It's the worst part of moving. Small chaos."

"I don't know about small," she said.

"After death and disease, moving is one of the most stressful things you can do."

"You should go on a quiz show," she said. "You'd make a bundle. Obscure facts."

"Maybe," he said.

She still wore the T-shirt with the Children's Hospital logo. The list of words, which he had printed from the stutter's website, sat on the kitchen counter. Rose Marie glanced at it, mouthed a word, then looked at Farrell.

"Tell me about that," he said. He gestured, with his head, to the logo on her T-shirt.

She shrugged.

"It's complicated. People get strange about it."

"Okay," he said. "Maybe you can tell me later. Is it a matter of trust?"

"Maybe," she said.

"You know," he said. "I bet with all that moving you aren't cooking. Let me make dinner."

"Can you cook?" she said.

"I know a few things," he said.

She drank a glass of white wine, which was like the distilled light of France, and she watched as he made linguine alle vongole, and a salad, which he put on the table in the small nook that had a view of her house.

"This is good," she said. "Wow. How do you know how to do this? It beats the Chinese takeout I've been getting."

"Trial and error," he said.

She took the plates from the table and put them in the sink, and when she came back, she hesitated at the list of words on the counter. Then she poured wine into each of their glasses.

"I have a little trouble s-s-sometimes. The list helps."

He wondered if she thought less of him, or as a sort of human fire sale.

"Honest, too," she said.

"I don't know about that," he said.

She kept on looking at him.

"So, what about that little scar in your eyebrow. There's been some rough trade along the line. Is that it?"

"A long time ago," he said.

"And so what do you do?" she said.

"I help people," he said. "You know, when they get into trouble."

"This is the right town for it," she said.

"That's what I've noticed," he said.

"You must know something about this town," she said. "Given your line of work."

"That's right," he said. "I know something."

"Maybe you could help me," she said.

"Sure," he said. "What are neighbors for?"

He gestured to the logo.

"What about that? Long hours?"

"It depends on how sick the kids are," she said.

"So, you work with sick kids?" he said.

"Yes. But, as I said, people get odd about it. A lot of times I tell people about the kids and then it's not the same. They don't turn away from me but they keep their distance."

"How sick are they?" he said, although everything about her suggested the answer, and so he wasn't surprised when she said,

"Terminal. They get bored, you know. You can imagine. Sitting around and waiting . . ."

She kept her eyes on Farrell. Was he another poser you met in California, not false so much as held together by desperation?

"Would you like to meet them?" she said.

"Yes," he said.

"Just like that?" she said.

He nodded.

"Okay," she said. "I'm going to trust you."

"It's your funeral," he said.

Then she gave him that two-hundred-watt smile.

"You sure you want to come?" she said.

"If I said I'll do it, I'll do it," he said.

He could see she was thinking, Is this man real, or does he just seem real? Farrell began to wonder about that himself as she kept looking at him.

"I'll come," he said.

"I'll call a day before I ask you to visit," she said. "To give you a little warning."

"What do you want me to talk about?" he said.

"Well, the kids like nothing better than trouble. Who doesn't?"

"Hmpf," he said.

"Is that hmpf, yes, or hmpf, no?" she said.

"It depends on the trouble," he said.

"I'm not asking you to get graphic," she said.

"I can talk around things," he said.

"What's your phone number?" she said. She took a drink. "I'm going to go finish putting my kitchen together, put lampshades on, break up some boxes, the last fodder for the recycling center . . . but I'll text you the kids' pictures so you can learn their names. It makes things easier."

She emptied her wineglass, stood up, leaned close to him, the smooth skin of her cheek touching his, and said, "You are probably going to be trouble. It always happens fast, doesn't it?"

"When it happens," he said.

"But what's a girl to do?" she said.

"There's always time to get out," he said.

"But we haven't even started," she said. "I think."

At the door she looked over her shoulder and said, "At least you can learn their names while you are brooding about whatever it is . . ."

"Hmm," he said.

"Hmm," she said.

Then she smiled.

The pictures came about two minutes after she closed the door to her house, and he scrolled through them on his iPad. She had included, for each photograph, a description of what was killing them.

Gerry, Catherine, Ann, and Jack. Somehow, Farrell had assumed that they would all look alike, bald, pale, sad. But Gerry had red hair, freckles, and while he might have been a little thin, Farrell would never have thought that he was sick. Or, no, no lies. Dying. Almost dead. Gerry looked directly at the camera and smiled, his eyes showing some deep awareness, which might have been pain or anger or intense wisdom.

Gerry. Okay. That was one name. He didn't want to walk into the room where Rose Marie met with these kids, and have to ask their names, or, if he did ask, he wanted to make sure that he didn't have to ask twice. What could make him look more like an idiot than having to ask a dying kid his name more than once?

Ann was blond with curly hair, but maybe this was the way it grew back after a bout of chemotherapy, that contradictory word, as though almost killing you was therapy. Farrell guessed that's what it took for the cancers that these kids had. Pancreatic cancer, for instance. Ann had that same expression of anger and wisdom and Farrell found himself looking into her eyes the way he did when he was at the top of a cliff and felt the attraction of that empty space below.

Catherine was dark, oddly beautiful, in that sick or not, she still had a sort of heroin chic, pale skin, dark hair, and the blue eyes of a model. She didn't smile as much as the others, as though her beauty, which she must have been aware of, was heavy or painful. Still, she had something Farrell couldn't name, knowledge, certainty, an awareness of something most people spent their time avoiding.

That left Jack, who had glioblastoma multiforme, a pediatric brain cancer that killed almost everyone who got it. He was a little cross-eyed, brown haired, thin, still smiling although it left Farrell with the sensation of being at the top of a roller coaster that was about to make that first long fall. Gerry, Catherine, Ann, and Jack. Farrell swiped from one to the other to make sure he had the names. Then he glanced at the clock and realized he had been looking at the pictures for a long time. What was it those kids had? Dignity and bravery.

* * *

The next day, his phone rang with Braumberg's ID showing. Farrell knew it was coming, but the memory of Rose Marie in his house and the display on the caller ID left a new, an unexpected dissonance.

Braumberg said, "You better get up there."

"Terry's house?"

"Yeah, Terry's house," said Braumberg. "And, get this, a mother of one of the girls is involved. A receptionist who works at Universal."

So there was more than one girl?

"Is she there now?" Farrell asked.

"I don't know," said Braumberg. "That's your job, right?"

Farrell had some cash in an envelope, and he put it in the pocket of his blue chambray shirt. He still looked like he worked for Outward Bound.

Rose Marie's presence from the day before lingered in the kitchen. Was it a motion in the air, a small change in the charge of the room, a vibration of some sort that was so frail that he wondered, Could I be imagining it? The air in the room seemed different, but it was impossible to say how it had changed. Now, though, the mood was going back to the way it usually was. Whatever she'd left drained away, and as it went, he tried to stop it by considering what she had told him about growing up in California, that her parent's house, in Hidden Valley off the Ventura Freeway, had simply vanished in a fire, the foundation like dust, the stink as intense as a bombed-out city. It smelled like a skunk. The loneliness, the emptiness of what had been left lingered, or she had grafted it into herself, which made her incomplete until she began to work with the kids who were sick.

THE LIGHTS OF THE VALLEY flickered and the air was scented with that perfect mixture of chlorine and eucalyptus. The Spanish style house with those ceramic half pipes on the roof appeared in silhouette, dark upstairs, the lights on in the living room. Farrell knocked on the heavy door, and while he waited his fingers touched the rough grain of the door, which had the pattern of trees in a jungle, all parallel, all dark.

"Boy, am I glad to see you," said Terry. That movement of his eyes from the valley below to Farrell and back again.

"Before I come in the house or even think about it," said Farrell. "We've got to get something straight."

"Sure, buddy, what's that?"

"The card. Did you get the c-c-card from Alaska?" said Farrell.

"What's the big deal?" said Terry. "Why the hard-on about a postcard?"

"Did you get it?" said Farrell.

"I got it," said Terry.

"I want to see it," said Farrell.

"We got another problem," said Terry.

"No. *We* don't have any problem. Unless you let me see the card," said Farrell.

"Okay, okay," said Terry.

He brought out the card and offered it. The picture was of snow-capped mountains, the color of them a little dim in the light that came from the door. A bear stood in front of the mountains, its face to the camera, eyes indifferent, or threatening. Not a grizzly, but lighter in color. A Kodiak. Even in the dim light the white snout showed. On the message side, it said, "All right, Big T-ster, I made it back in one piece, so you don't have to worry anymore. Warm weather here. Love, Mary Jones." The dot above each *i* was either a heart or a smiley face. Postmarked in Anchorage. Note written in purple ink. Farrell held the card, flipped it over, then put it in his pocket.

"Hey," said Terry. "Why are you keeping that?"

"Let's go inside," said Farrell.

"I want to keep the card," said Terry.

"Let's go inside," said Farrell.

The living room still had the white sofas and white carpet with deep pile, the glass table, the walls covered with posters of movies that Terry had been in, a map of Hollywood, a painting of a nude woman on the young side, and a map of London, where Terry had studied at the Royal Academy for six months.

Terry sat at the glass table, where a copy of the *Los Angeles Times* was open to the photograph of a man, Karicek was his name, who had been arrested. Farrell hesitated over the photograph and the headline that said, "Man Arrested on Morals Charge. Young Women." Terry folded the newspaper, a little huff of air coming out of the pages as they settled on the table. Farrell guessed the mugshot in the paper made Terry more tense, his eyes shifting from the window to the two young women, or girls really, who sat on the sofa.

The first one had a stage name, but then mothers here gave stage names at birth. Portia Blanchard had a nose job and looked like she was a throwback of some kind with her hair dyed red, her nose with a piercing. She wore a tight white tank top and a red skirt.

She held her hands together, looked away, licked her lips, bit them, and then tried to look at Farrell with a glance that was cold and arrogant, as though she had a natural cunning and didn't tolerate anything or anyone getting in her way unless they were looking for trouble. It left her, in this elegant room, with a perfect expression of the parochial nature of her desire. That is, parochial by Los Angeles standards, which, Farrell thought, were pretty definite. Snobby, condescending, fueled by a belief in glamour and beauty, as though these were the real gifts of the gods. And now, she had the air of something else, not terror, not yet, but surely she was worried. Farrell swallowed.

"Who's this?" said Portia.

"My producer sent him," said Terry. "He's going to make it all right."

"We'll see about that," Farrell said.

Portia's eyes were a storm-cloud blue, and maybe she had a number of different colors for her contact lenses. What's more convincing than a dark, brooding stare?

Charlene was the other young woman. She was blond, seemingly wholesome, sort of sweet, really, if you didn't do more than just glance at her.

"What's his name?" said Portia to Terry.

"Just plain Mr. J-j-jones," Farrell said.

"That's a funny name. No one is really called Jones," she said.

"Where's the mother? Wasn't a mother supposed to be here? Yours, Portia?" said Farrell.

Farrell glanced at Terry's hands, his brittle movement, his look of getting close to the worst precipice.

Farrell had the impulse to feel sorry for Portia and the other girl, since neither one knew what they had gotten themselves into. He touched the card in his pocket from Mary Jones.

"Charlene?" Farrell said.

"How do you know our names?" said Portia.

"I talked to my producer about you," said Terry. "I guess he talked to his guy."

He gestured to Farrell.

Beyond the window, the lights in the valley had a cold, starlike twinkle.

"Where's your mom?" Farrell said.

"We thought we'd leave her out of this," said Portia.

"Oh?"

"Yeah," said Portia. "Maybe she can't handle some things."

"Maybe we want to do something on our own," said Charlene.

"Get out your phone and call your mom," said Farrell to Portia. "Tell her to come right over."

She looked one way, then another, at Terry, the Valley, the blue hump of the San Gabriel Mountains.

"Go on," said Charlene.

"Why?" said Portia. That little quaver in her voice.

"This guy," said Charlene. She gestured to Farrell. "Can take care of things . . ."

"Shut up," said Portia. "Let me think."

The sullenness between them was the variety that only two scared teenagers can have.

Portia sighed. Then she tapped a name in the contacts section of her phone, sulked while she waited, and then said, "It's me. You better get up here. We're talking things over."

So, thought Farrell, the mom doesn't need the address.

"She'll be here in twenty minutes. Traffic, you know."

"That's fast," said Farrell. "Where do you live?"

"North Flores. West Hollywood," said Portia. "You can make it in fifteen minutes if you're lucky."

Particularly if the mother was waiting for the call, thought Farrell. At least she was on her way. They sat like strangers in a waiting room. Terry said the weather was nice for the fall, and then they decided that it was better not to say anything.

The girls glanced at one another as a way of communicating, but more than anything else it was an argument conducted by glances, by a grimace now and then, with a shake of a head. Charlene sighed, gestured to Farrell said to Portia, "I think he can help . . ."

"I don't know," said Portia.

She squirmed in her seat.

"There's some problem? Beyond you and Terry?" said Farrell.

"I told you to shut up," said Portia to Charlene.

Terry blew up his cheeks and then exhaled between his lips, as though he was trying to whistle and couldn't quite make it. His lips were too dry.

Farrell considered Charlene, a nice kid who at least remembered what it was like not to be in this room with whatever surprise was coming.

"Remember," said Portia to Terry. "We didn't want to do anything."

"We'll get it straight," said Terry.

The knock on the door came with a light tapping, as though it was a sign for a private club.

Farrell opened the door.

Cherry Blanchard stepped inside. No greeting aside from a glance. She appeared as though she had come to the end of the line. Plastic surgery wouldn't do any more for her. Another one who had come to the end of hope. Or delusion. Farrell shook his head and wanted to comfort her, but he knew that would have to wait. Still, in other circumstances Farrell would have understood, even been sympathetic. He would have bought her a drink and agreed that this was a tough town. Breasts enlarged, probably lips augmented, a new nose. But of course, while each feature was enhanced, the underlying pattern, or face, or whatever it was that you are born with was still there, a sort of medical pentimento. You could see Portia there.

"This is Plain Mr. Jones," said Portia.

Cherry put out her hand.

"Nice to meet you," she said. "You're the one to talk to, right?"

"Yes," said Farrell. "Aren't you at Universal?"

He didn't say a word about her being a receptionist. Which, Farrell thought, must have been hell on earth for someone who had come to LA with ambitions and then was left to sit behind a desk and watch people she saw in *People* walk by without so much as a glance.

"Yes," she said.

"Good," Farrell said. "So, let's get things straight."

"Okay," said Cherry.

"Now the first thing is no one tells a lie," Farrell said. "If you do, I will give you a warning, and the second time, I'm walking out of here."

"I never lie," said Cherry.

She ran her hand through her hair, which had been bleached and streaked.

"So, what are you going to do?" said Cherry.

"I really don't know yet. A lot depends on you. How did the girls get up here?" Farrell said to Cherry.

"We hitched," said Portia. She sniffed, touched her nose piercing. Farrell reached for a box of Kleenex and held it out. Her sullenness had a ray-like quality, focused on Farrell. Mixed with that dread. It was as though she thought the way to deal with the world was to show it how superior she was. That ought to keep them in line, the losers. At the same time, she had a contradictory mood, since she was afraid that the world was about to fall in.

"Cherry?" Farrell said. "Is that right?"

"If that's what they say," said Cherry. She looked at Farrell with same sullen air, as though it was genetic.

"Didn't you drive them up here?" Farrell said. "And why didn't they drive themselves? Don't they have a license? Aren't they sixteen?"

"Just learner permits. They'll get a license soon. If they said they hitched up here, they did."

"And you think it's a good idea to let sixteen-year-old girls hitch-hike in this town, up, say, Laurel Canyon?"

"Probably not," said Cherry.

"So, you drove them up here?" Farrell said.

"Why, how could you suggest such a thing . . . as though I'm participating . . . or was participating . . ."

"I said, no lies. That's the first warning," Farrell said. "Now, did you drive them up here or not?"

Cherry looked out at the valley below.

"Yeah," she said. "I drove them last night. They hitched up here tonight. What I said was true, though, they just have learner permits."

"In a month," said Charlene.

Portia looked at her as though Charlene had bad breath.

The valley shimmered there like every false hope imaginable.

"We aren't going to have any problems here, are we?" said Terry.

"We could go to the cops," said Portia.

Cherry nodded.

"No," Farrell said. "You won't."

"Why not?" said Portia.

"Listen to him," said Charlene. "Just listen."

"Why don't you just shut up," said Portia. "I'm warning you."

"So, when were you the boss, huh?" said Charlene.

"Don't be so lame," said Portia.

"So, you were here last night?" said Farrell.

"Yeah," said Charlene.

"Is that right, Terry?" Farrell said.

"Well, yeah, in a manner of speaking," said Terry.

Farrell looked at him.

"All right, all right," he said. "They were here last night. Let's not make a federal case out of it."

Farrell swallowed.

"So, we've been talking over what we want," said Portia.

"I thought you were supposed to leave things like that to me," Farrell said to Terry.

"In this new movie, we want some lines," said Portia.

"Five lines apiece," said Charlene.

"And a card," she said. "In the titles with our names on it."

"The script has already been done," Farrell said.

"That's not our problem," said Portia.

"We haven't talked about money," said Charlene. "Yet."

"So, it's five lines apiece, a separate card, and some unspecified amount of money."

"Yeah," said Portia. "Unless we think of something else."

"How does that sound to you, Terry?"

"Five lines isn't so much," he said.

A copy of the script was on the glass table, the top of which seemed to have a film from dust or from use, like dirty glasses. Portia picked up the script and flipped the pages.

"There's a place . . . let me find it . . ."

The house had slight noises, the hum of the high-end freezer in the kitchen, the occasional car on Mulholland, some slight burble in the plumbing, a dripping in the shower . . . Portia read the script.

"You know, Terry, you have a six-a.m. call . . ." Farrell said. "You remember that, don't you? Maybe you should get some sleep."

"I better stay around," he said. "To see what's what."

"So, Mr. Jones, do we have a deal?" said Portia.

Her eyes were like the color of the Aegean at noon.

"My jeans are stained," Portia said.

"Stained?" Farrell said.

"From him," she said. Her head bobbed toward Terry. She kept that gaze on Farrell.

"So, this morning you went home, left the jeans there, and came back?"

"That's right, Mr. Jones," said Portia. "We won't wait long before going to the cops."

"I don't think you want that," Farrell said.

"No?" said Portia. She bit her lip.

"It's up to you," Farrell said.

"Jesus," said Terry. "What the fuck are you saying?"

Portia looked like she was about to burst into tears, then pulled herself together. Farrell felt sorry for her, but that didn't change things too much.

"I want this fixed soon," said Portia.

"Yeah," said her mother.

"The problem is that you lied to me once," said Farrell. "Now I have to do a little work to be able to know what's going to happen."

"It wasn't much of a lie," said Cherry.

"You think so?" Farrell said.

"Yeah," she said.

"Maybe I don't want anything to do with this . . ."

"What?" said Portia. "What?"

That look between Charlene and Portia.

"Why are you so frightened?" Farrell said.

"We're not frightened," said Portia. Then she bit her lip again.

"Listen to him," said Charlene. "He can fix this . . ."

Portia stared at the hills in the distance, which were covered with the bright specks of houses and streetlamps. The effect was like a dark hump covered with strings of white Christmas lights. Peregrine, Charlene, Portia, and Cherry sat around that table. The valley shimmered with that beguiling promise, as though it was a charm that could be invoked.

"Take out your phone," Farrell said to Portia.

"Why?" said Portia.

"Call the cops."

Portia's eyes were like that moment just before dark, when the sky is blue on the verge of black, when the first star is visible.

"Dial," Farrell said. "Call the cops."

Farrell got out his phone and called a number.

"Howie? It's me. Sorry to bother you at home, but I'm going to need some legal advice. Can you call me back when you get a chance? We're going to have to do that thing we did a couple of years ago. You know, when we fixed that kid? The Youth Authority bit. So, call me."

Farrell hung up. Portia stared back. Just tell me, thought Farrell.

"Go on," he said.

She sat there, her hatred seeming to feed on itself. Peregrine ran his hand through his hair. Charlene trembled.

"Look," said Charlene to Portia. She gestured to Farrell. "This guy can fix things. You know? Maybe he can take care of it?"

"Be quiet," said Portia.

"You think it's just going to go away?" said Charlene.

"The first thing is to tell me what else went on here," said Farrell.

Terry cleared his throat and glanced at the valley. Still, Portia's fingers were shaky, too, and she blinked again to stop tears from showing.

"Let's trust him," said Charlene.

"I'm going to handle this," said Portia.

"Let's take a big, deep breath," said Cherry. For a moment she looked like she was at her yoga class.

"So," said Farrell. "You aren't calling the Hollywood station. That means something."

"What the fuck does it mean, Mr. Jones?" said Portia.

"You remember I said the first rule is that you don't tell me any lies."

"Everybody lies," said Portia. "It's how money is made. If we didn't lie, three-quarters of the money in the world would disappear tonight. So, what's the big fucking deal? Tough guy?"

"Mr. Jones," Farrell said.

"Mr. Fucking Jones," said Portia.

"So, let's talk about what happened," said Farrell. "And the first thing is . . ." He looked at Portia. "You're lying to me."

She stared back. Charlene started to cry.

"I bet there was someone else here last night when your mother brought you up to see Mr. Peregrine," said Farrell.

"Men like Terry are so easy," said Portia. "They go into a kind of trance when they start thinking about it."

"Oh, come on," said Terry.

Cherry opened her bag and took a roll of Dramamine from it, put two in her hand, and swallowed them dry. She really did look like she was going to throw up.

"Well?"

Charlene cried harder now and Peregrine handed her the box of Kleenex.

"Don't get snot on the couch," he said.

"If I were you," Farrell said to Terry, "I'd keep my mouth shut."

"She was a runaway," said Portia.

"So, there was someone else here that night?" Farrell said. "Is that what you are telling me? That's the problem, right?"

Charlene looked up with the saddest face in the world: a sixteen-year-old girl, cheeks streaked with mascara, who knew that the promise she had counted on, the effect of youth, and what she could get with it, were up in the air.

"Do you know that or are you guessing?" said Portia.

You poor kid, thought Farrell.

"Tell me about her."

"We met her on Sunset," said Portia.

"She was hungry," said Charlene. "Desperate for a shower. Wanted to shave her legs. So, we took her home to my house and put a pizza in the microwave, let her have a shower, let her shave her legs, gave her some makeup. She looked great. She had something special. Really had it."

"British," said Portia. "Had an accent, like, you know, like some snooty cunt."

"So she came along when we came up here to see Terry," said Charlene. "She was so beautiful. Black hair, and I mean black. Blue eyes. Bone structure to die for."

"Cherry?" said Farrell.

"Yeah," she said. She looked at the floor. "I guess there was another girl."

"Guess?"

"There was another girl, okay?"

"So, where is she?"

"He," said Portia, moving her shoulder toward Terry. "Gave her a drug. She got a little woozy . . ."

"Terry," he said. "What was it? Flunitrazepam?"

"A roofie," said Terry. "She didn't seem to need it though."

"She threw up," said Charlene. She held a Kleenex in one hand, just a ball now. "Made a mess in the bathroom."

"And you slept with her?" Farrell said to Peregrine.

He nodded, although he looked down at that lush carpet. No one should try to take away from me what's mine, Peregrine seemed to say. No one. Why, I'll rip the sun out of the sky. . . .

"Did she have any identifying marks?" Farrell said. "Tattoos? Scars? Marks of any kind? Birthmark?"

"What do you want to know for?" said Portia.

"That's my lookout," Farrell said.

"She had a tattoo in that sort of German script," said Portia.

"Gothic?" Farrell said.

"Yeah. Like on fancy German beer bottles. Just above where her pubic hair would be, that is if she didn't shave. She was a Jesus freak or something."

"Maybe," said Charlene. "Pretty skanky for a Jesus freak."

"The tattoo said, 'Blessed is the man that heareth me, watching daily at my gates, waiting at the posts of my doors.' Proverbs something or other. Chapter. Verse. Whatever that stuff is. Small type. Arranged like a fan."

"Nothing else?"

"Listen," said Portia. "We want our lines."

"What do you want that British runaway for?" said Cherry. "She's not here. She's gone. So, she's not part of this at all."

"But you're not sure where this girl is. What was her name?"

"She called herself Patricia Melrose," said Charlene.

"I don't know how she got here from England," said Portia. "She was a runaway. Who cares where they go?"

"But you're uneasy about her," Farrell said to Portia.

She shrugged.

"Terry took care of her . . ." said Portia.

"How was that?" Farrell said.

"He took her to the doctor."

Terry looked at the floor, then nodded.

"Yeah," he said. "Yeah."

"She didn't look too good," said Charlene.

"We had to carry her out to the car," said Portia.

"Then you waited for Terry to come back?"

"Yeah," said Portia. "She didn't look too good."

"I know a doctor," said Terry.

"Where is she now?" Farrell said. "Doesn't she want a couple of lines and her own card?"

"No," said Terry. "She was more into other things."

"Who knows what happens to people like that," said Portia. "You know how many runaway girls there are in town? If we could just get our lines, we'd forget the entire thing."

"That's the best thing," said Cherry. "And we can forget about everything else. All this stuff about a runaway."

"So, you don't want to go to the police because of Patricia," Farrell said. "If that's her name."

Portia shrugged.

"Just get us our lines," said Portia. "That's all that counts."

"I'll work on it," Farrell said. "Cherry, are you going to drive them home?"

"Yeah," she said. "If we're done."

"You're going to help, right?" said Charlene.

Farrell stared at her.

"I don't like that look," said Portia.

"I'm not feeling so good," said Peregrine.

"So, what now?" said Portia. Cherry put her hands together. Terry bit his lip.

"I'll be in touch," Farrell said. "You should have told me about the British girl." He was about to walk to the door, but stopped and said, "Where do you live?"

"Santa Monica," said Portia. "Is that a crime?"

He looked at her again, then wallowed and said to Terry, "Walk me out."

Farrell got into his car, rolled down the window, put the keys in the ignition, but took a moment to consider the lights in the valley. He had looked at them when he had parked with a girl from high school and had felt that warmth where they had touched. Her shirt still had the scent of laundry detergent clinging to it.

Terry stood next to the rolled-down window.

"You act in a couple of movies and you can't trust anyone," he said. "Like these girls. You know what they did? They fucking stole my toothbrush. Tortoiseshell handle, great bristles, comes from Italy. I just used it, and I go back into the bathroom and one of them has taken it. I missed it this morning. Like they just had to have a souvenir or something. You can't even trust them for a fucking toothbrush. You see how it is?"

Terry shrugged with self-pity and the unfairness of things.

"And then," said Terry. "I have to get some bum to straighten things out . . ."

"What?" said Farrell. "What did you call me?"

"I don't know," said Terry.

"A b-b-bum," said Farrell.

The lights in the valley had an icy glitter, like Christmas tinsel left in a gutter.

"This isn't easy," said Terry.

Your life is hanging by a thread and you say that to me? thought Farrell. He considered how good it would feel to let the sharks have Terry. That close, thought Farrell. If you only knew how close you are.

"I didn't mean it really," said Terry.

"Sure, sure," said Farrell.

"You forgive me?" said Terry.

Farrell winced, in spite of himself, looked away, and then stared at Terry's handsome face.

"Let's just get this taken care of," said Farrell.

"Look at those lights in the valley," Terry said. "You'd be surprised what people do for a view like that."

"No, I wouldn't," said Farrell.

Terry tapped his head against the roof of the Camry.

"Makes you think where you came from," said Terry. "And how much you don't want to give it up."

"I know where you came from," Farrell said. "And what you did when you first came here."

"You mean being a fluffer?" said Terry.

"Yeah," said Farrell.

"All right," said Terry with a kind of furious despair. "I was a fluffer and other things, and you think I'm going to just walk away?"

They looked at the valley where those lights shimmered. Farrell considered what fluffers did, or how they kept men ready in the movies made in the Valley, even in the days of Viagra and Cialis. He imagined Terry's head sinking into a man's lap.

"In West Virginia," said Terry. "Everyone had bad teeth. Broken refrigerators on a back porch. I worked in a gas station and when a guy in a Jaguar came in, he gave me a look. You can tell. That's how I got to New York."

He stared at Farrell for a long time, and the look of a tough kid from West Virginia was right there, as though he was in a trance.

"So, tell me about the doctor," said Farrell.

He went on staring at Farrell with that same look, as though he was holding a piece of two-by-four with a tenpenny nail in it.

"She was sick, throwing up, and she was pale."

"Who is the doctor?" Farrell said.

"What does that matter?" he said. "Doctors do me favors. I'm discreet about them. Okay?"

Discreet?

"And what happened?"

"He gave her a shot of Narcan, and she snapped right out of it. Asked for a cigarette. Bang."

He went on staring at the valley.

"Really beautiful," he said. "The first time I saw it, I thought, I'm home."

The scent of eucalyptus lingered in the air.

"You remember what I said about lies?"

"Of course," said Terry. All false charm now, like a beauty queen.

"So, she snapped out of it," Farrell said. "Then what?"

"I took her to Musso & Franks. Right by the Wax Museum," he said. "Got her a chicken pot pie. She said it didn't compare with fish and chips, but she ate it. Then I dropped her off on Sunset. God knows where she went from there."

"Where on S-s-unset?" he said.

"Must have been at Doheny," he said. "Yeah. Doheny. I gave her fifty bucks."

"And you remember about the lies?"

"Yeah," he said. "You're my pal. There's nothing to worry about her. You know what she said about those two?" He gestured to the house, where Portia and Charlene were. "She called them dumb clunges. I don't even know what that means."

"It's not polite," Farrell said.

"That's what it sounded like," he said. "I used a condom with her, you know, her being from England with all those Pakistanis. Who knows what she had?" He glanced at the valley. "So, there it is. Last seen on Sunset at Doheny. Okay? No problems there."

He swallowed.

"No one is going to take anything away from me. That's it. Do we understand each other?"

"I understand," said Farrell.

"That's good," said Terry. "Sorry about the bum stuff. It just came out."

"Listen to me," said Farrell. "Don't you touch those girls. Don't . . . hurt them. Leave them alone. Do you hear me?"

"Do you think I'm dim?" said Terry.

Farrell started to roll up the window, but Terry stopped him.

"I have to stay centered," said Terry. "You know?"

"Sure," said Farrell.

"I think of my hero. James Dean. Now there was an actor, right? The myth. He was fearless. That's the thing. He didn't give a shit."

"He died pretty young," Farrell said.

"Yeah, but what a way to go," Terry said. "Flat out in his Porsche. A Spyder, right? Going like a bat out of hell. He just disintegrated. Right out into history. Never to be forgotten. Have you seen my Spyder? It's around back."

"Some other time," Farrell said.

Terry turned and went back to the house, but hesitated, head turned toward the valley. He appeared as a silhouette, silent, still, as though cut from black paper, but he had an air of regret, or mystification, as though everything he had wanted, no matter how superficial, meant more than he could say, although he seemed to feel it like some physical pain. The mysterious ache he gave off lingered like the scent of eucalyptus.

Farrell knew there was one thing, and only one, that he was going to do, had to do. That meant as much to him as Terry not giving up what he had. Farrell knew the one thing was to find the British girl.

7

CHARLES DENT HAD AN OFFICE on Cahuenga Boulevard in a suite of rooms that were arranged in a building that was a cube. Stairs on each end and an entrance in the middle that lead to a square court-yard in which there were some palms so healthy they must have lived on Miracle-Gro. They were surrounded by hibiscus like the brightest red lipstick. Farrell went up the stairs in the courtyard and into a hall that was like something from a dream. All the doors were the same. The plaques by each door had been made at Staples, and they were for an accountant, a financial adviser, and a psychologist, Werner Jacobs, PhD. Next to the shrink's office was the door for Charles Dent.

Dent was in his late twenties, had a haircut like someone in an ad for Brooks Brothers, and wore khaki pants, a blue shirt, and high-end Nikes. If you saw him in the street and were then asked to describe him, you would come up with a blank.

"Hey, Farrell," said Dent. "Come in. Sit down."

In the office there were two enormous monitors, an ergonomic keyboard that was shaped like an upside-down V, and a wireless mouse. Also ergonomic. Two iPhones, a pad of paper, and a pencil. An ergonomic chair.

"Shhh," said Dent. He had a water glass in his hand, put it against the wall, and then pressed his ear against the base of the glass. "You can hear the shrink next door . . . wait a minute."

Dent listened. Then he shook his head.

"It's like a soap opera. You wouldn't believe what people do. Just un-fucking-believable."

"I've got an idea," said Farrell.

"Well, you've got an unfair advantage," said Dent. "This woman here . . ." He gestured to the wall. "Well, first . . ."

"It's all right," said Farrell. "I can guess."

Dent put the glass down.

"Well, she always comes at this time on Tuesday. I'll get the next installment in seven days."

Farrell put an envelope with cash in it on the desk in front of the enormous monitors.

"Something you are interested in?" said Dent. "Credit card records, phone records? Bank records . . . ?"

"Not right now," said Farrell. "But I wanted to make sure everything is okay."

"Yeah," said Dent. "Everything's fine. All wars were won by offensive weapons. You see? All that computer software, all that security stuff, well, there's always something they forgot, or an item they never dreamed possible . . ."

Farrell raised a brow.

"You should get a job in the film biz," said Farrell. "You know, for the production design for a picture about a hacker . . ."

"Yeah," said Dent. "I should. They are always wrong . . . you know, they always show hackers that have a mess of tattoos, long hair, fat, and they live in some rathole of a cellar . . ."

He shrugged.

"It reminds me of the movie version of writers. In the old days they used to always be ripping sheets of paper out of a typewriter and making a ball of them. Now it's typing on a laptop, and then deleting it. Same schtick, over and over."

"What do you think it's really like?" said Farrell.

"Staring out the window," said Dent. "Yeah. That's probably what it's like. Same thing with hacking. You have a piece of software set up to grind out a password, and you look out the window while you wait . . ."

"I guess," said Farrell.

"There's no guessing," said Dent. He picked up the envelope. "Thanks."

"Sure," said Farrell. "I'll be around."

"At your command," said Dent.

* * *

In the morning before the fog burned off, the color of the air was like the fur of a gray cat, and the fountain at the Hollywood Bowl splashed with that same low tide hint. The concrete bench was cool, and the cars moved with that stop-and-go aspect of LA traffic. Either too fast or too slow, but never just right. Farrell guessed that traffic had held Braumberg up, which probably left Braumberg with the essential LA mood, anxious to get someplace but stuck.

It wasn't that Braumberg was going to do something stupid. But Farrell understood that Terry's trouble affected Braumberg as a variety of physical irritation, as though insects had gotten into his clothes, or as a maddening itch. Braumberg knew that he shouldn't scratch it, but how was he going to stop? He understood panic as confinement. It wasn't Braumberg's intelligence that Farrell had to address so much as his impulsiveness, and how can you make someone sit still when they are dying to scratch?

One of Farrell's first jobs for Braumberg had been to escort an actress to Las Vegas. Braumberg didn't trust just anyone with the cash to pay the actress's gambling debts, since, for all he knew, if he gave the money to the woman, she might start in at the craps table. Again. The actress, Amy Branshaw, and Farrell took the plane from Burbank, a direct flight to Las Vegas.

Her skin took light so that it glowed and made the camera love her. But she didn't want to have her breasts done, and so she was wearing a brassiere with two balloons, one under each breast, and they could be blown up with a little tube that was hidden beneath the balloons. Halfway to Las Vegas, the airplane lost cabin pressure.

"Look," said Amy Branshaw. "Jesus, what am I going to do?"

Her breasts, or rather the balloons under them, were swelling and her blouse was taut at the buttons. They were getting bigger. She put her arms over them, but she looked like a running back carrying an enormous football. The other passengers turned to look.

"Are you going to do something or not?" said Amy. "Have you got a knife?"

"When was the last time you took a knife on an airplane?" Farrell said.

"Do something," she said.

Farrell had a cup of coffee, with a plastic stick to stir the powdered creamer. He bit the tip of the stick to make a point. The button on her blouse was easy to push out of the button hole, and then his hand went into the warmth beneath the balloon. The heat was keenly intimate, oddly soothing, and suggested the fragrance of her skin. A steward stood in the aisle and stared. The first balloon sighed as air came out, and the breast went down. But the other required some pressure to pierce it. The steward said, "Passengers are not allowed intimate embraces when in the air."

When Farrell ran into her again, at Sotto on Pico Boulevard, she had taken a moment to recognize him, but then she blew up her cheeks and winked.

Today, Braumberg no longer had the energy to consider a disguise. No faux carpenter outfit. He arrived in his black Armani sweater, his dark pants, his snakeskin cowboy boots. His eyes were set on the temple of the Vedanta Society across Highland.

Braumberg sat down next to Farrell and said, "What's in your box?"

The lid of the pillbox had a picture of *The Birth of Venus* on it, and Farrell took it out of his pocket, opened it, and offered it to Braumberg. It had three sections: one for Ativan, one for Xanax, and one for Klonopin. Braumberg took a Klonopin. Panic. The effect of Terry Peregrine all over.

The scale of trouble worked by itself, as a natural law. The increasing budgets for the pictures Sam Braumberg was making gave him a producing fee right off the top, and as the budgets increased, so did the pieces of it that people making it received, that is if they were lucky enough to get paid a percentage of what it all cost. But as everyone knew, more money meant more risk, and a lot more money meant a lot more risk.

This collided, as far as Farrell was concerned, with the fact that the trouble people got into was worse than even a few years before, since people faced a downward spiral, whether it was jobs going to China, robots replacing people on assembly lines, or the excesses that fame seemed to license with its larger, more intense scandals. A little while ago, a scandal could have involved drugs. That was child's play. Just consider, Farrell thought. Gerbiling. Or what kind of trouble was available in a world where, online, a man could advertise or at least suggest that he wanted to be killed and eaten? Farrell felt this as if being on a ride at an amusement park that left him a little dizzy, although he walked around as though he was taking a sobriety test. A sensation that was hidden, but still keen for all that.

"Are you seeing someone about that stutter . . ." said Braumberg.

"I do exercises," said Farrell. "Words that catch me."

"What's a hard word?" said Braumberg.

"F-f-f-fury . . ." said Farrell.

But it's not the words, thought Farrell. It's the things I can't say.

"Yeah," said Braumberg. He bit his lip. "So, tell me. Have the girls gone to the cops?"

"Not yet," said Farrell.

"Ambition," said Braumberg. "They start young out here."

"The girls are threatening to talk to the cops, but I don't think they will. You've got another problem."

"Explain it to me," said Braumberg.

"Something else happened. The girls are scared. Terry is lying."

"Goddamn it," said Braumberg.

"A girl from England was there. Probably sixteen, too."

"And?"

"She had a bad reaction to something Terry gave her. He says he took her to the doctor, but no one knows where she is," said Farrell.

"So, if she's gone, there's no problem," said Braumberg. "Right?"

No, thought Farrell. Not by a long shot.

"You better get ready for something else. The girls want a couple of lines a piece. In this new picture. So, you better set that up," said Farrell.

The fountain continued to splash.

"The director is Derek Profonde," said Braumberg. "Comes from central Europe. He's an asshole. They're *artists*. If I ask, he will think I'm off my meds. And interfering."

"Did you tell him about Peregrine?" Farrell said.

"Do you think I was born yesterday?" said Braumberg. "Of course not. That's why I came to you, right?"

Braumberg was sweating and he had a sheen on his forehead. It looked almost icy.

"Shit," said Braumberg. "Why the fuck did I ever hire this prick?"

"Which one?" Farrell said.

Braumberg put both hands up in the air, as though to say, *all of them*.

"I've got deals in almost all the territories for distribution," said Braumberg. "And with a little luck we will break even on production costs before the shooting is done. The first weekend will cover distribution costs. If it's done right. The rest is pure gravy. Now, you see how close I am?"

"Yeah," Farrell said. "Profonde has got to add two parts, just a couple of lines for each character. Two sultry teenage girls. Four lines altogether. Two for each."

"The writer isn't going to like it," said Braumberg. "She's got this, you know, edge to her."

"Tell her it's from the marketing people. They've seen the dailies and want some teen item. Tell her they think they've got to have a couple of sulky teens in it."

"Shit," said Braumberg.

"Is that a yes?" Farrell said.

"Okay," he said. "And if I can't swing it here we will get something else that is shooting now."

Braumberg put his hand in the greenish water of the fountain.

At the light in front of the fountain, a pickup truck with a rusted bed and what looked like recap tires rear-ended a Porsche with a crushing *thump*. Braumberg and Farrell had a moment of euphoria at the recognition of someone else's trouble. Like having a tooth suddenly stop aching. The driver of the silver Porsche got out. She was a blond woman with dark glasses, who wore tight blue jeans, a tight tank top. Her beautiful lips were probably swollen with a shot from her plastic surgeon. Farrell stared at her shoes.

"You see those?" Farrell to Braumberg.

"What?"

"Her shoes. Snakeskin. Python, I think."

"How do you know what a python skin looks like?"

"Trust me," he said.

The woman put her hands on her hips and leaned into the window of the pickup truck, where a Latino man stared straight ahead. No, he didn't have an insurance card. The cops arrived and one of them, in a perfectly pressed uniform, the black pants having an edge like an envelope, got out and looked around as though he wasn't ready for another one of these. The woman yelled and gestured at her car. Wasn't that evidence enough? Did anyone know what she had gone through to get that fucking car? The driver of the pickup truck sat behind the wheel. The woman in the snakeskin boots sulked in the middle of the road.

"Jesus," said Braumberg. "LA."

Honking in the street. The woman screamed. The man behind the wheel of the truck said nothing.

"When are you going to see them again?"

"As soon as I find the British girl," said Farrell.

"Why don't you leave that alone?" said Braumberg.

"I don't see it that way," said Farrell.

"So when are you going to start looking?" said Braumberg.

"As soon as this fog burns off," said Farrell.

They sat in the burbling of the fountain and in the stench of exhaust from the cars on Highland.

"So, how did it go with the vending machine business?" said Braumberg.

"Some lowlifes are s-s-shaking me down," said Farrell.

"It figures. You can't even try to pay taxes in this town," said Braumberg.

"Russians," said Farrell.

"Let me tell you something," Braumberg said. "I tried to make a picture in Moscow and the thugs were so bad, so threatening for every day we tried to shoot, we had to give it up. And in India where we tried to shoot a movie it was even worse."

Farrell shrugged.

"I'd be careful around them," said Braumberg.

"That's my problem," said Farrell.

The fountain made a burble, which had a hint of a death rattle.

"Here's your hope," said Farrell. "The only way the girls can get what they want is to be quiet. If they go to the cops, it's over for them. Once they start talking, it's over. Do you have their last names?"

"Terry told me. Portia Blanchard. Charlene Klauski," said Braumberg.

"How do you spell Klauski?" said Farrell.

"Klauski. K-l-a-u-s-k-i."

Farrell kept his eyes on the Vedanta Society temple. How soothing that pink architecture was.

"Things aren't as simple as they used to be," said Braumberg. "The above the line costs are nuts, but then the below the line costs are, too. And that is before distribution costs."

"I've got to go," said Farrell.

"Okay," said Braumberg. "Jesus, look at the Vedanta Society. Is that a cult?"

"No, the Vedanta Society is legitimate. You know who used to go there? Aldous Huxley. He used to be a regular."

"You mean the *Brave New World* guy?"

"Yes," Farrell said. "The *Brave New World*. If he had only known."

"At least we don't grow people in bottles," said Braumberg.

"It depends on what you mean by bottles," said Farrell. "Look, I've got things to do."

Farrell drove that gray Camry up Highland to the Cahuenga Pass, and in the rearview mirror saw that Braumberg was waiting, as though in answer to a prayer, for a fast rate of absorption.

* * *

The cold fog of Los Angeles in October got into his bones in a way that left Farrell with the sense that he was chained by it. Just try to get away, it seemed to say. Farrell went home by way of the Cahuenga Pass to Mulholland toward Laurel Canyon. On the way he considered his current circumstances as something out of Dante, where he was at about the Seventh Circle, which meant that he had at least two more levels in the bank. What kind of trouble could eat two entire Circles of hell in one bite? Then he considered that antsy movement of Terry Peregrine's hands, the look in the eyes of those girls, the uncertainty about the British girl, and the uneasiness he had over the card from Mary Jones.

Farrell had a pile of copies of the *Los Angeles Times*, which he kept in a cast iron rack in the hall of his house. Every couple of weeks he bundled them up and took them to the recycling center, where he almost felt like he was wearing a disguise. The good citizen who recycled newspapers, used a shower that saved water, and kept a composter. Now, he found the paper from the day before, took it to the kitchen and put it on the table, glanced at the headlines, and turned to page six. He found the story about a man who had been arrested for sleeping with fourteen-year-old girls. Karicek, Frederick, or Freddy. He had been arrested six times before, but he had still been on the street. The man had come from West Virginia, worked odd jobs, as a gardener's assistant and a pool man. Terry had been spooked by this article. He hadn't wanted Farrell to see that his eyes were drawn back to the story in the paper.

He took out his iPad and turned it on. That little Apple logo appeared, and Farrell wondered about it. A bite of the apple was the myth of death. Then he pulled up Peregrine's address with Google Maps, Satellite View. Farrell guessed that Peregrine didn't have the patience or the presence of mind to do a good job, which, of course, meant that he probably didn't go very far from his house. And, Farrell guessed, Terry had wanted to get back to the girls who were waiting. Maybe Terry had been thinking about what they would do. Maybe he had some new ideas he wanted to try with them.

The satellite view showed the few places that looked likely . . . not as many as there used to be. The canyons were smaller, too. As difficult as it is to change the landscape, the developers had done just that when they ran out of land. The solution had been to fill the canyons with dirt and build on that. Sometimes after a brush fire and a good rain, the dirt washed away and the houses built on it slid downhill. But, after all, thought Farrell, this was LA, and nothing was certain, not even the place where your house was built.

How close to Peregrine's house should he begin to look? Farrell guessed the dirt shoulder on Mulholland would be useful, since it would show if a car had stopped there, but then how many people stopped to look at the view, or how many kids pulled over to smoke a joint and dream about what was coming?

After lunch was the best time to look when the morning fog was gone, although Farrell liked the fog, too, since the Camry fit so perfectly into the shark-like mist. Still, the mist made it harder to see what was left in a canyon.

Farrell knew the canyons. At the end of the academic year, when he had come back to LA from Berkeley, he delivered newspapers, the *San Fernando Valley Pink Sheet*, which was a throwaway. He borrowed a station wagon to do the job. The bales of papers, bound with wire, were delivered by a flatbed truck to the sidewalk next to a strip club. The club had been built to look like a log cabin, on Ventura Boulevard, and its charm, if it had one, was a variety of long-term seediness. Sometimes, in the morning, one of the dancers wobbled out on high-heeled shoes, not too drunk, but not sober, either. Usually, Farrell would give a drunk stripper a paper. One of them, with purple hair, said, "Thanks. I let my puppy crap on it."

Farrell made a sort of bench out of a bale of newspapers and a sort of desk out of another bale, and then he put another, open bale on the desk and folded a paper into thirds, put a rubber band around it, and threw it into the back of the station wagon. With the car so full that it was dangerous to drive (with a pile of papers flowing into the passenger seat and a pile right behind), Farrell drove through the streets of Studio City and, steering with his knees, he threw the papers out of two windows, one on the driver's side and one on the passenger's side. It looked like a sort of destroyer, shooting depth charges, although it was just pink papers that landed on lawns.

It didn't take long for Farrell to realize the facts. The paper was a throwaway, already doomed. Only five people actually subscribed, and also fifty-three people had threatened to sue if the paper was ever thrown on their lawns again. These houses were known as stops. So, after a couple of mornings that started at 5:30 a.m., it was obvious what Farrell should do.

He folded five papers and then put the untouched bales of papers, still held together with wire, just like a bale of hay, into the station wagon. He drove to the five houses where the subscribers lived, delivered the five copies, and drove into the hills. The problem, of course, was how to get rid of the bales of paper that no one wanted. Farrell drove on Mulholland, west toward the beach, until he found a canyon with a steep edge, and then pushed the bales in. He was back in bed by 8:00 a.m. This landscape, in its details, soon became as familiar as the bed he slept in.

The trouble began with the distribution manager of the paper and the Los Angeles Fire Department's Fire Inspector. They showed up one morning when Farrell was folding up the five copies that he actually delivered. Then they drove him into the hills and showed him the slag of bales in the canyon Farrell had chosen. They could have pressed charges, but, instead, the manager just fired Farrell. The canyons were still familiar, although with some more houses.

Farrell got in his car and turned out of the privet hedge. He guessed he'd start five hundred yards from Terry's house and work toward the beach, but he thought that a half mile from the house would be as far as Terry would go, high and paranoid and with the girl with the pubic tattoo in the back seat.

Terry probably drove west on Mulholland toward the beach, since the canyons were less developed that way, although you never knew with people like Terry. All swagger, but when push came to shove, maybe he was tougher than you'd think. That look of murderous rage, so carefully hidden in that faux charm, didn't come easily to most people, or it came only to a few. And yet Terry had another quality, which was that his toughness was an intermittent item, useful when he had the upper hand, to be avoided at all costs when he was risking something. Still, the distance from Terry's house was determined by something far beyond courage. No one, thought Farrell, should underestimate what Terry would do to keep what he had. It was possible, too, that Terry could be cunning. Maybe it would occur to him that the best thing was to go a couple of hundred yards and then look for a place. Right there.

Farrell was sure of one thing. The girl, if Terry had done this, wouldn't be too far down a canyon. Terry wouldn't be willing to drag anyone through the brush, especially if it was filled with rattlesnakes. Or could be. A likely possibility. And there were plenty of rattle-snakes in the canyons, as Farrell knew by experience.

Farrell had a parking permit on the dashboard, a card that said, LOS ANGELES DEPARTMENT OF WATER AND POWER. The first possible place was about two hundred yards away from Terry's house. There, Farrell pulled over, got out of the car, and stood at the top of the canyon. Brush and manzanita, but he'd have to walk into it, since it would take some looking to find a sixteen-year-old girl who had been shoved under some woody clutter. He pushed into the brush, and as he did so he held the stiff branches back to find a way in. He glanced at the fecal colored dirt, in those shady places under a man-zanita. Here and there a handful of soil rolled down the slope with an almost animate quality, as though something was skittering away. No buzzing of a snake, nothing but that mixture of brush scent and exhaust from the freeway.

He looked in every possible place with a five-hundred-meter radius, but then Terry's ambition and panic, or his ability to endure, might allow him to go farther, even if he was panicked. If you didn't mind being a fluffer, what wouldn't you do? Was being a fluffer a matter of enduring what was necessary?

Terry had to make sure that no identification was left on the girl, and maybe, although Farrell wasn't sure about this, since the clothes the girl was wearing might have come from Charlene or Portia, they might have even helped dress her before he took her to "the doctor." Was that right? Terry could have said that the girls didn't want to be involved, and so was the British girl wearing any of their clothing now? Was that why the girls were so frightened? Or, would it be just Terry who would take the girl's clothes off and throw her naked into the brush? Then it would just be a matter of finding a dumpster to get rid of the clothing, shoes, a handbag. Terry knew that a case of underage sex was one thing, but that a dead girl was another. The way Terry saw it, Farrell knew with absolute certainty, is that if the girl wasn't around, the problem was solved.

Farrell knew these were just guesses. In fact, Farrell knew that any combination of details could be involved, since at any moment that night Terry could have panicked, left the job only partially done, or hardly done at all. This was the problem with panicky people who got frightened halfway through what needed to be done. Nothing was less trustworthy than a terrified man. Or less predictable.

What was that quality that hung like still, ominous air?

Farrell was not a religious man, but he realized, as he stopped and waded into the brush, that he was praying that he wouldn't find her. Maybe it was just his contempt for Terry, for the unseemly aspect of the people he helped, but he knew, too, beneath it all, precisely what he would do if he found the girl.

The canyons were mostly a deep V, lined on each side with brush and manzanita, with some eucalyptus here and there, which had that Musterole-like miasma. That medicinal trace left Farrell with a momentary and still-precious sense of innocence.

The Department of Water and Power sign on the dashboard was his excuse for being here, and if anyone asked he'd say he was making a survey to upgrade power lines so that they would resist even earthquakes, which everyone up here would be glad to have done. The fires had always burned here, but since houses were built in new places that naturally burned, it was just more anxiety for LA. Not the city of Angels, but La Ciudad del Miedo, the city of fear. The fires and a hard earthquake were just a matter of time. Farrell had grown up not far from here, and the sound of a eucalyptus exploding was like the memory of some recurring nightmare.

More brush, some game trails, more heat, and the cloying effect of working his way through plants that curved over his head, not like a romantic bower, but something else altogether. Then, when he came out to the shoulder of the road, where cars had parked and shoes had left marks, he realized he was up against a new variety of loneliness. A surprise, since he thought he had been knowledgeable about this, but the scale of the unknown for what he felt or could feel and for what he would find left him with the sense that every object, whether distant or close, highway, tree, car, road, grid of streets in the valley was now illuminated by fear. Hadn't he learned how to handle that? No, he realized. Not anymore.

By six in the evening, rush hour had begun. Farrell thought it wasn't good to be seen looking along the side of the road. What happened if someone else found her first? There was a guy, someone might say, in a gray Camry poking around. . . . The risk was personal, since if someone identified him, or if the cops came to him, what was he supposed to say? He was taking a leak? Admiring the view? I see, a cop would say. Bladder problems, huh? What about this dead girl?

The roses in the arbor around the door of his house were the last of the fall flowers, and this made the perfume all the more intense. Isn't the end always the most memorable? Isn't that why we pay attention to a man's last words?

He took a shower.

Rose Marie called and said, "How are you doing?"

"Fine, g-g-great," he said.

"Tell me another," she said. She waited a minute. "What are you doing tomorrow?"

"Work in the afternoon, but in the morning when it's foggy, I've got nothing to do."

"Good, good," she said. "Will you come tomorrow? I need help."

"Okay," he said. "In the morning."

"Sure," said Rose Marie. "When it's foggy."

Alone in his bed, the scent of eucalyptus lingered, and the rustle of the sheets, as he turned one way and then another, was a dim reminder of the crackle of a distant fire, and then keen memory of a eucalyptus exploding, the top with a red and yellow and red shape like the flame at the top of a candle. Then the sound, *Bang*.

In the morning, the clothes in his closet hung like different versions of himself. To be an inspector for the Department of Water and Power, he had dressed like someone who worked there. The same outfit would be right, he guessed, for visiting with Rose Marie's kids.

The postcard with the picture of the bear was stuck on the refrigerator by a magnet, a little trout. Farrell put the trout aside, with a click, and turned the card over. The writing seemed loopy with its smiley faces and hearts for the dots above each *i*. It said, "All right, Big T-ster, I made it back in one piece, so you don't have to worry anymore. Warm weather here. Love, Mary Jones." Farrell flipped the corner of it with his thumb and put it in the pocket of his Patagonia jacket.

8

Rose Marie drove her red Subaru, and Farrell sat in the passenger seat. He didn't want to stutter in front of the kids, and so he swallowed once and then again. Still, he took the card from his pocket and looked at the bear and then the message.

"What's that?" said Rose Marie.

"A postcard," said Farrell. "How old are your kids? Teenagers, right?"

"That's right," said Rose Marie. "What's on your mind?"

He put the card back in his pocket. He rolled a shoulder.

"I don't want to stutter," he said.

"They won't mind," she said. "They've got other things to worry about."

***

And, she considered her own worries. Or at least she confronted a mysterious sensation, which was that the edges of her sense of self had become a little fuzzy, and at the same time, in that haziness, she discovered a desire or maybe it was already a fact that this was a matter of blending with the warm understanding of the man who sat next to her. How could there be any awakening, since she had thought she was beyond anything like that. She didn't know if the need for that warm comfort and the fact of melding with someone else was more surprising or terrifying. Or the terror came from not being sure that he felt it, too.

* * *

In her warm, inquisitive glance, Farrell considered the search for the British girl, the trash he saw at the side of the road, used condoms and their foil packages, empty pints of vodka, candy bar wrappers, cigarette butts, and empty baggies that had still had the dust of marijuana inside.

The sprawl of the UCLA medical center had the appearance of all such vast institutions, not quite as ominous as prisons, but not completely reassuring. The clutter of buildings made Farrell aware of how alone he was. Their haphazard arrangement suggested the unleashed forces behind such things, the arrival of money, the advancement of technology, as though these developments were alive and not necessarily interested in specific people. Things that you couldn't control, or that just happened to you. LA all over, Farrell thought.

One building with a flat roof, boxlike and made of aluminum, already pitted by the salt air from the Pacific, had taken a hard to define but still noticeable hit from an earthquake. Still usable but not perfect, as though something weighed on it.

A new parking lot was in front of the buildings, the lot surrounded by orange netting as a temporary fence, and at the entrance sat a guard in booth who issued parking tickets and took money. He wore dark glasses and reminded Farrell of the scent of formaldehyde. Beyond the booth sat a backhoe with the teeth of its bucket against a new pile of dirt. Rose Marie licked her lips, checked her makeup in the rearview mirror, then kept her eyes on the distance. Outside the car they stood in air that had a hint of the Pacific, which was only a few miles away.

"So, it's glamour you work with," Rose Marie said.

"Not glamour, no, not exactly," he said.

"But fame, the movies, things like that," she said.

"It may not seem like it, but Hollywood is still like a mill town. A lot of people in town work there. From electricians to seamstresses to hairdressers."

"But that's not your part, right?"

"No, that's not my part," he said.

In the parking lot she was so quiet that she seemed to be a sponge for sound. Farrell took her hand, and she squeezed back. Something new. They were holding hands. She said, "I'm counting on you."

"I get it," he said.

"I bet you do," she said. "That's what's strange."

The revolving door of the hospital moved a visitor into the lobby with a mechanical shove. This way, my friend, it seemed to say. Here you are.

"You're going to have to perform," said Rose Marie.

He nodded.

"Okay," he said.

He swallowed.

The room, on the fifth floor, was a school of sorts. A window looked over the clutter of the medical center, the buildings for surgery, oncology, tropical disease research, brain research (Farrell thought he could hear the banging of MRI machines), chronic pain management, and others.

The kids' room had a whiteboard, and on it earlier in the day a teacher had drawn shapes for geometric theorems, side angle side, angle side angle, and a right triangle with boxes at each leg and the hypotenuse.

"What?" said Rose Marie.

Trigonometry… Hubcap, humbug, lemon…tight fit…tight.

"Trigonometry," he said.

"You can leave, if you want," said Rose Marie.

"No," he said. "I'll stay."

The classroom had the lingering odor of a place where kids got sick, like dirty socks mixed with Lysol.

"Do the kids get sick here?" he said.

"Sometimes," she said. "Not just throwing up, but they can have a seizure, too. Have you ever seen one?"

"I've dealt with epilepsy," said Farrell.

They walked into the middle of the room.

"Gerry, Catherine, Ann, and Jack," Farrell said. "Are they coming soon?"

"You've got a good memory," said Rose Marie.

Like tracks left in the dirt of the shoulder off Mulholland. Something left under some brush.

"I wish I had a surprise for them," Farrell said.

"That's one of the things these kids never get. They know what's coming. They've given up on surprises." She kept her eyes on his. "I guess you'll be all right. You don't look like you scare easily."

Not until recently, he thought.

"Just charm the kids," said Rose Marie.

The kids hung at the door for a moment, dressed in street clothes, jeans and shirts and flip-flops, Gerry with red hair and freckles, like an advertisement Farrell thought for Boy Scouts and merit badges. Although here, close up, Gerry's eyes swept over Farrell with a piercing awareness. And just like that, Farrell thought, What the fuck is wrong with me? Why so vulnerable? Why on the verge of tears?

He smiled.

Catherine was a little more thin than in the pictures, far along in the heroin chic look, and when she came in she gave Farrell that same knowing glance, as though she had an advanced understanding of what people really struggled against, or that she had spent time in some demanding discipline, as in a monastery where residents take a vow of silence. It's not that she knew anything about what he had been looking for off the shoulder of Mulholland, but she recognized the mood that came from it. Hope mixed with terror and anger. Farrell was more certain about the need to find the British girl than ever.

Jack wore a baseball cap to the side, just like the young men in South Central LA. He glanced at Farrell and came in with a sort of swagger, as though he was going to be able to bluff his way out of glioblastoma multiforme by sheer attitude and defiance, which, Farrell guessed, was about all he had. Ann was on edge, and the least friendly of the lot. Her dark eyes didn't greet him.

"This is my friend Quinn Farrell," said Rose Marie. "I thought he might talk to us about the movie business."

The kids nodded, although Catherine dared him to look into her eyes. It wasn't so much that she was distant as above Farrell in some way. If you made a fool of yourself in front of a kid this sick it's not something you were likely to forget.

Catherine seemed to exist with pure awareness. Farrell was comforted by this, since at the moment, in the presence of the mood here, fatigue seemed to drop on him like a net. It came from lies, distortion, and nonsense that he had to deal with. Here, at least, there would be none of that.

"Let's sit down," said Rose Marie.

The classroom chairs had been arranged in a sort of semicircle with two in the middle, one for Farrell and one for her. She got some boxes of juice out of the small refrigerator and passed them out, giving one to Farrell with a straw sticking out of it. He thought this was the kind of straw they probably used around the mirror at Terry Peregrine's house.

Rose Marie glanced at Farrell as though to say, All right. You're on. Charm them.

"So," said Catherine. "I know something about Hollywood. My parents had a neighbor in Woodland Hills. Before they dumped me here."

"What did the neighbor do?" Farrell said.

"Pretty sketchy stuff, it seemed to me," she said.

"Like what?" he said.

"He was a kind of host for people who came to town, you know, a new actress from Germany, a director from Poland, a film distributor from Argentina. He showed them the sights."

"Sights?" he said.

"Yeah, you know. Do I have to spell it out?"

"No," he said. "No. You really don't."

"So, you know," she said.

"Yeah," said Farrell. "You can say that. What was the neighbor's name?"

"You think you know him? Gerald Stiller. Ring a bell?"

He shook his head.

"So, is that kind of thing you do?" she said.

"No," he said. "Other things."

"Like what?"

Her eyes were violet and blue, and Farrell recalled the eyes of Mary Jones.

"Let's get to know one another," he said.

"Sure," said Catherine. "Let's get to know each other. But don't think we are going to let you off the hook about it."

"Sure," he said.

"Give him a chance," said Rose Marie.

"We'll give him a chance," said Jack. A scar, as though made of pink bubble gum, ran below his turned around baseball cap.

"Turn on the charm," said Ann.

"Do you think you can charm us?" said Catherine. "Go ahead."

"Try," said Gerry. "Yeah. See what you can do."

"You're double teaming me," said Farrell.

"We do it all the time," Catherine said.

"Let's talk about animal sounds," Farrell said.

"You've got to be kidding," said Catherine. "You want to talk about that?"

"Yes," Farrell said.

"So, what about animal sounds?" said Gerry.

"I knew a woman who spoke Russian," Farrell said.

"Who was that?" asked Catherine.

Rose Marie kept her eyes on him. After all, they hadn't known each other for very long. But to Farrell the time didn't seem brief at all.

"Just a friend," Farrell said. "So, I asked her what sounds animals make in Russian."

"Aren't they the same?" said Ann, her golden curls bouncing a little as she turned from the window and looked at Farrell.

"Well, in America, what noise does a pig make?"

"*Oink, oink, oink*," she said. "Isn't it the same?"

"In Russia, it goes, *khriu, khriu, khriu.*"

"What about donkeys?" said Catherine. "Here they go *eee-ah, eee-ah.*"

"Not in Russia," Farrell said. "In Russia it goes *ooah, ooah.*"

"Seriously," said Ann.

"Yes," Farrell said. "That's what they say."

"How about ducks?" said Catherine. "Don't they go *quack, quack, quack?*"

Rose Marie kept her eyes on him.

"In Russia, a duck goes *krya, kyra, kyra.*"

"*Krya, kyra, kyra?* Not *quack, quack, quack* . . . ?"

A man in green scrubs went by the open door, and he glanced at Rose Marie as though to say, If you need help, I'll be right down the hall.

"Are you making this up? I bet you make a lot of stuff up," said Catherine.

"What about a rooster?" Farrell said.

"Everyone knows that," said Gerry. "It goes *cock-a-doodle-do.*"

"In Russia it goes *ku ka ryeh ku.*"

They laughed, and Rose Marie's gaze finally came across. Just wait, it said, until I get you alone.

Jack had been quiet, but the animals in the barnyard pulled him in, too.

"All right," he said. He looked right at Farrell, as though he had him dead to rights.

"I've got you. What about a cow. It goes *moo, moo,* right?"

"You're right," Farrell said. "The same."

Jack looked around as though he had just set things right. See, he seemed to be saying. Just listen to me. But all of them laughed, and then they laughed harder because they were laughing, and Rose Marie was so glad to see them laughing she laughed, and then Farrell did, too.

"*Krya, kyra, kyra,*" said Ann. "You've got to be kidding."

"What about a coyote?" said Catherine.

"Like when?" said Farrell. "They make different sounds."

"How about when they are searching for something?"

"For instance?" Farrell said.

"Roadkill, something like that."

"Or something that died in the brush. Deer are always dying in the hills."

"Sometimes it's roadkill," said Catherine.

"Yeah," said Gerry. "But they don't leave a deer in the road."

"What happens?" said Ann.

"Someone drags it to the side of the road or pushes it into the brush," said Catherine. "You have to report it to the cops and all of that."

"Not always," said Gerry. "Not always. Sometimes they just leave it there."

"What do you think?" said Catherine to Farrell.

"Maybe someone drags a deer to the side of the road and sticks it in a bush because they don't want any trouble. As you say. Better to hide it."

"Maybe the birds show you where it is," said Catherine. "You can see them circling, can't you?"

"You could watch for the birds if you were trying to find the deer," said Gerry.

"But you know, sometimes they just drive over it until it's flat. Like a smear," said Catherine.

"There's a phrase for that," said Farrell.

"Yeah?" said Catherine. "Like what?"

"A s-s-sail cat," said Farrell.

"A sail cat?" said Catherine. "*A sail cat?*"

The kids laughed and Rose Marie did, too.

"Well," said Catherine. "It will never be the same. If I ever get out of here and see one of those . . . sail cats."

"I'll keep an eye out for birds," Farrell said. "When they are looking for something, they seem to spiral around, like water going down the drain."

"Yeah," said Catherine. "Like little bits of ash. In the water." She went on looking at him. "Are you looking for something?"

Those eyes lingered on his face and he felt it almost like a slight breeze. Farrell thought of the sky along Mulholland. He hadn't seen any birds but he would be careful later, this afternoon or tomorrow.

"No lies," she said.

He nodded.

"Sure I'm looking for something. Isn't everyone?" Farrell said.

Catherine kept her eyes on him.

"What about your stutter?" she said.

"I do some exercises," he said. "Sometimes it seems like a little man is there. I can't shut him up."

"We've all got some problems here. And they aren't sometimes." Catherine said. She pursed her lips as she thought.

"People come in here all the time and they think they know about our problems. They don't. Not until you are in the spot I'm in. They can go fuck themselves," Gerry said.

Outside in the hall a man polished the floor with a machine that had a large, circular brush, and it made a little whisper as he moved it back and forth.

Farrell took the postcard out of his pocket, the picture side held to the kids. The bear's face was turned to the camera, the expression utterly blank, as though it was peering from some other world.

"What's that?" said Gerry.

"Let me see it," said Catherine.

She took it with a slight, haunting tug.

"Good looking bear," she said.

"Where is it postmarked?" said Gerry.

"Alaska," said Catherine.

"I'd like to ask you about it," said Farrell.

"What do I know about bears?" Catherine said.

"It's not the bear," said Farrell.

"Or what do I know about Alaska," said Catherine. "Lot of trees and fish and caribou, right?"

"I guess," said Farrell. "But look at the message."

Catherine flipped the card over, glanced at the loopy script, then held it up for the others. They passed it around, as in some kind of parlor game, and then it came back to Catherine.

"What do you think?" said Farrell.

"Phony," Catherine said. "Too many smiley faces and hearts. No one uses both. And this T-ster thing. No one says that. It's so ten years ago. You know what I mean?"

"Yeah," said Farrell.

"So, it's just phony."

Farrell put out his hand.

"Thanks," he said.

"Sure," said Catherine. She handed it back. "No girl writes like that. This Mary Jones. Is there really someone called Mary Jones? Name sounds funny, too."

Farrell put the card back in his pocket. For a moment the scent of the shoulder of Mulholland came back, the glitter of the torn foil packets, the sad, shrunken condoms, and the cigarette butts with lipstick on them.

"You want to hear what actors we like?" said Ann.

"I like Matt Briely, Sandra Gottfried, Billy Nash, and that new one, that French girl, Michelle Mercredi," said Catherine.

"Yeah," said Ann. "And Terry Peregrine."

Farrell looked out the window at the clutter in the parking lot.

"What's on your mind?" said Catherine. "What are you going to do if you find something . . ."

"Maybe I'll come back to tell you about it," Farrell said.

"Sure. But don't wait too long," she said.

Farrell turned to her.

Catherine crumbled her juice box and threw it in the trash.

"All we want is honesty," said Gerry. "We aren't just fucking with you for fun or making you feel guilty because you aren't going to die."

"I'm going to die," Farrell said.

"Not so fast as us, I don't think," said Catherine.

"You never know," Farrell said.

"Well, you better work fast," said Catherine. "If you want our advice."

Farrell thought he could smell the chemotherapy on her breath. He looked out the window. Clutter of new buildings, a crane like a prehistoric bird, that toxic California sky, and all of it combined into a physical hint, like the landscape of a dream, that things just couldn't continue. But who was changing, him or the world?

"Maybe it's time to call it a day," said Rose Marie.

"Not on your life," said Catherine. "I've got something to say. To him."

"Okay," Farrell said.

One of the kids sucked at the last of the juice in a box, and the sound was like the last pool of water going down a drain.

"I've got one hope. If someone promises me something now, they will keep the promise when I'm dead. That's it," said Catherine.

"So, what's the promise?" Farrell said.

"I want you to promise that when the time comes, when you find what you're looking for, I want you to think of me. And do . . . the right thing. Do you promise?"

The crane outside began a slow, sluggish movement, like some unstoppable thing.

"Yes," Farrell said.

"Yes, what?" she said.

"That I'll keep my promise."

"To whom?" she said.

"To you," Farrell said.

"No," she said. "To all of us."

There it was, that long, cool, and oddly moral reach from the dead to the living.

Farrell nodded, and she nodded back.

Then she started laughing.

"Just kidding," she said.

"No, you aren't," Farrell said.

She looked right at him.

She started crying, the tears on her face like rain on a window.

"Good luck," she said.

"Thanks," Farrell said. "You, too."

"Oh, I'm beyond luck."

They stood and shook Farrell's hand, which the kids liked. A lot of people wouldn't touch them because they thought cancer was contagious.

Outside, Rose Marie and Farrell got in her car and sat there for a while and faced the hospital's mismatched architecture, the dust from the new parking lot, and the guard in the booth. The guard's movement was mechanical, which Farrell felt as oppressive, as though this was an outpost for disease.

"I should have warned you," said Rose Marie.

Farrell's hands shook.

"How do you warn someone about them . . . ?"

"That's the problem," she said.

"Sure," Farrell said. "They are the only honest people in town." She nodded.

"Well," she said. "There's me."

That smile.

"Thanks," she said. "They liked it. I can tell."

Rose Marie turned out of the parking lot and drove east, toward Sunset and Laurel Canyon.

Rose Marie parked in front of her house and sat with the attitude of being unsure just where she had been. She pulled on the brake with a slow consideration, and then looked at Farrell for a long time, and in that glance, he detected a promise she was making, too.

"Luck," he said. "It's never there when you need it . . ."

"Yeah," said Rose Marie. "I hope you aren't depending on luck." She swallowed.

"Maybe there's more than luck involved," Farrell said.

"What's that?" she said.

"There's me," he said.

Rose Marie went into her house with that swaying of her hips, that upright carriage, and Farrell stood in the drive while she walked away.

In his kitchen, he began to put the postcard on the refrigerator with the trout magnet, but he held it for a moment to see the smiley faces, the hearts, the loopy script. Then he sat at the table in the booth by the window, where the paper was opened to that picture of Karicek, the man who had been arrested. Farrell ran his fingers over the face, the nose, the bones in the cheeks, and the eyebrows.

Of course, he knew that going to the police was dangerous, but he guessed it was time. Time to be careful, though. Charm, cunning, and patience.

9

FARRELL THOUGHT HE WOULD SEARCH a little more to the west on Mulholland, but even though the fog was burning off, he hesitated. Yes, the air was clearing, but time was growing short. He wondered if taking a chance would give him a sense of clarity, if only because it concentrated what he had to think about.

The cop was almost like a relative. Shirushi had arrested Farrell when he was young and they had improbably stayed in touch. Making her a kind of cousin, or something. She was Japanese American, restrained, but precise, although she had a sense of humor and liked to crack a joke by raising a brow. Oh? she liked to suggest, do you think I buy that? Shirushi wasn't much older than Farrell, and they met for a meal or drinks a couple of times a year.

At seventeen, Farrell had stolen a motorcycle every Friday night and had thrown it in the Los Angeles River every Sunday. The Los Angeles River is not much more than a large cement trench, and since he dropped the motorcycles in the same spot, he had made a pile of motorcycles. Shirushi had dark eyes and a brooding presence, as though she was always working out an integral equation. She had been standing next to the pile of motorcycles on a Sunday evening when Farrell put the last one over the edge of the embankment at the top of the LA River. That had been a long time ago, and Shirushi, with her short hair, cut so that it was just beneath her ears, was now a detective. After she had arrested Farrell, she had arranged things so that he had only done a month in the California Youth Authority camp in Malibu during August so he could still get to Berkeley as a freshman in the fall. Farrell had to wear boots with lead in the soles when he was in Malibu, since this guaranteed he would not try to escape. Not unless he wanted to do it in bare feet through that landscape.

He called Shirushi from his kitchen. The bright colors of the Paris Métro map left him thinking, If I could only get there.

"Why, Farrell, it's been awhile. How are you doing?" said Shirushi when she answered her phone.

"Fine, fine," he said.

"Uh-oh," she said. He could almost see that raised brow.

"What's wrong?" he said.

"Your voice," she said. "You sound like the first time I arrested you. You remember those motorcycles?"

"How could I forget?" he said.

"Is that a compliment or a plea?" she said.

"A compliment," he said. "I'd like, you know, to say I trust you."

"I'd be careful about that," she said.

"How about a late lunch? Spur of the moment. The usual place. My treat. In an hour," Farrell said.

"Short on time, too," she said. "Well, well."

Shirushi liked Fuyuko's, a sushi restaurant in Santa Monica. It had a view of the Pacific, and if you met in the afternoon, as now, the Pacific appeared as a platinum sheet. Shirushi was tall, had slight freckles over her nose, and now that she was a detective, she sometimes wore silk dresses, which clung to her with a gleaming liquefaction. But only when she was in the mood. Often she wore jeans and a T-shirt, which is what she wore today.

Now, she sat with her back to the door and her face to the ocean. She took his hand with that cool, but still friendly, touch.

"I have a favor to ask," he said.

"All right," she said. "But let's, ah, define the rules of the game."

"Just a favor," he said.

"Well, we can talk as friends, in a purely personal way. Or you can talk to me as a cop. So?"

"A little of both," he said.

She ordered sushi, salmon, crab, octopus, and a glass of beer, and she made a little bench from the paper wrapping that the chopsticks came in. A little piece of origami. She had taught Farrell to do this in the past, and now he made a little bench, too. It was a small thing, but he hoped it was a way to establish an old friendship, or at least a common pool of experience.

"Sometimes you can't see things clearly," she said. "For instance, you know why I'm sitting with my back to the door?"

"No," he said.

"In the days of the samurai, a host always sat with his back to the door, since if an assassin came in, the host, with his back to the door, would die first."

"I don't think we have to worry about that," he said.

She raised an eyebrow.

"And do you know why samurai swords don't have a blood gutter? The blood gutter makes a slight hush when the sword is being swung, and if you are sneaking up behind someone and swinging the sword you want it quiet."

"You aren't your usual cheerful self," he said.

"You aren't either," she said. "Your voice on the phone was an illustration of Shirushi's First Law. Sooner or later you will find the thing you are afraid of."

The sushi had the taste of the ocean, and the wasabi burned. She kept her eyes on Farrell.

"So, what are you working on?" she said.

"Are we still talking as friends or as my friend the detective?" said Farrell.

Her eyes, for the moment, were set on the piece of salmon on sushi rice. She dipped it in the sauce with wasabi, perfectly lifted it to her mouth, and ate it with the ability of someone who knows how pleasure should be drawn out.

"More friend than cop," she said. "But, if I were you, I'd be careful."

The wasabi made his eyes water.

"Why don't you give up sex crimes?" he said. "After all, you can take your pick now, can't you?"

"Yes," she said. "But with sex crimes sooner or later someone always gets killed."

She pushed her hair behind one ear, her black eyes, not like coal but like the depths of a well, made her expression so attractive as to exert a kind of gravity.

"All right," she said. "Enough foreplay. Before we get to the favor, you have to do something for me."

"What's that?"

She smiled, just brushed her fingers over his hand. An artery throbbed in her neck, with a slight, almost invisible pulse. She shifted on her seat.

"How much do you contribute to the Santa Monica Police Benevolent Society, or to, say, Tommy Black, you know, the guy who runs supervised detention, when he needs financial help? A house he wants to buy, having his kids' teeth fixed, something like that?

You know, so that when you call him, he can give you a detail or something."

"Now, you wouldn't want me to be indiscreet," he said.

She stared at him as though she had the key to a hotel room in her handbag. He wondered where she kept her sidearm. And if flirting was a part of her being a very good cop.

She raised an eyebrow. Then she took a piece of tuna, dipped it, and put it into her mouth. He took a bite, too, keeping his eyes on the small, almost invisible artery.

"I help out," he said. "I've helped Tommy. A donation helps."

She shrugged. "The thing about cops," she said. "Is that we aren't as stupid as you think."

"Does Tommy Black tell you about me? When I ask him for help? Is he making me into a rat who pays him? A confidential informant, who gives *him* money?"

"You wouldn't want me to be indiscreet, would you?" she said. She took another bite, then a drink of the cold beer to go with the sushi. "What's the favor?"

"There's a man, Karicek . . ." said Farrell.

"I know who you mean," said Shirushi.

"Can you check his DNA profile against someone?"

"That's privileged information," she said.

"I'm asking a favor," he said.

"You may think I don't know what you do," she said. "But you have to understand that the best thing is not to get involved in a pissing match with a skunk."

"Who's the skunk?" he said.

"Could be me," she said. "Could be people who keep secrets. Could be all kinds of people. Some more dangerous than others."

He looked down at the sushi boat, at once cute and oddly bizarre.

"The studio lawyers, who have irregular connections, production company lawyers, the people who work with them, the investigators. The newspapers. TV. Web gossip sites. Here's the way it is. It can be a real mess. And, there you are, exposed, and people get curious."

"I understand," he said.

"So, I might let you get away with the occasional ... irregular resolution of something. But these things can blow up. And you might end up holding a bag. A very big bag."

"Would you help me?" said Farrell.

"A few motorcycles are one thing, but ..." She shrugged. "If you think I don't know a lot about what you do, you are mistaken. Not everything, but I could go to work."

"So you want something, too?" said Farrell. "It can't be money, can it? Not that."

"No, not money. Just remember me. If something comes up." She smiled again.

He wrote *Terry Peregrine* on a napkin and passed it over.

"Karicek and this guy," said Farrell. "You already have a sample from Terry. In some database somewhere."

"Yes," she said. "*Maybe* I can do that. But you have to remember me. A reliable tip is always useful. A moment where two birds can be killed with one stone."

"They aren't birds," he said.

"I know," she said.

"If I didn't know better, I'd think you were dangerous," he said.

She expertly and with exquisite delicacy picked up her last piece of tuna, which she put into her mouth. It wasn't so much eating as something like a promise. Yes, he thought. She really is dangerous.

"You want to know the secret of police work?" she said. "You don't chase someone down. You just wait for them to do the same stupid thing a second or a third time ... You know, Farrell, after all these years, the least I can say is that I warned you."

"Well, that makes me feel a lot better," he said.

The waiter put the check on the table. Farrell picked it up, glanced at it, and took some cash out of his pocket, and put the bills in the little tray.

She slipped her card under his fingers.

"That," she said, pointing to a hand-printed number, "is my cell, which you've got. The other is a landline at my house."

The silver film on the ocean made the surface appear burnished.

"Thanks," he said. "It's always nice to see you."

"Don't be too sure," she said. That same smile. "Don't worry about the dead. They've been taken care of. It's the living you have to worry about."

"I'm not so sure about that," said Farrell.

"So, you believe in ghosts now?" said Shirushi.

"In LA, you'd have to be crazy not to."

10

On Laurel Canyon on the way to Mulholland the flow of traffic was steady. Rusted clunkers trailing smoke like a black feather boa, trucks, Porches, a vintage Rolls. And of course, lots of Camrys.

He widened his search this time. It seemed to Farrell that he had underestimated the desperation. Maybe Terry had more guts than he had given him credit for, but then maybe it wasn't guts so much as the realm were deviousness turned into obsession. Terry could just blink at you and tell you, "That girl? No problem. Everything's going to be all right." Not batting an eye. Was it the lying or the coldness that was the worst?

Farrell pulled up Terry's address on his iPad and examined the terrain within a half-mile radius. Then a mile. The landscape near Terry's house didn't have that many places, and he'd already searched them and come up empty. Or, was that wrong? Had he hidden the British girl in his house and then waited to move her? Farrell thought this was unlikely, but then with this scale of liar, anything was possible.

The sky was clear and there weren't any birds circling over anything. Then he thought of Catherine, and that glance in her eyes. Still, Farrell didn't want to go out as far as Sumatra Drive, and if he didn't go that far, he was left with the small streets that went toward the Valley, on the north side, or toward Hollywood, on the south side. Would Terry have taken one of those? More houses there, but more privacy, too, since there were places with a lot of brush.

Maybe it wasn't guts, but cunning. Guts would mean he could drive almost to Malibu on Mulholland, but cunning meant he could have gone a half mile and stopped behind someone's swimming pool. Cunning meant he knew the girl would be found. Guts meant he hoped that she would disappear. So, which was it? And why hadn't Farrell asked the obvious? How long had the girls had to wait for Terry to get back?

At the side of the road, in front of a wall of that brownish scrub, the dust of the shoulder, Farrell stopped and considered the possibility that Mary Jones was out here, too. How long had it been? Three weeks or so, maybe more. And how could she be identified? Farrell wasn't even sure she really came from Alaska, and then, if he tried to find out about her, he'd have to face any number of young women in Alaska who ran away to the Lower Forty-eight every year. And that supposed a missing person report was filed for each one. This, surely, was not the way it worked. So how many just slipped away, unnoticed or unreported?

Farrell had a box of latex gloves on the passenger seat. He put them in the glove box. If he was stopped, he didn't want to explain them.

From Mulholland, the Valley was obscured by the smoke that hung in the Los Angeles Basin, and it often seemed that the mood of the place was shown in the air. Farrell knew the job at hand was to bear down, to stop imagining things, but the difficulty was that imagining things was precisely how he worked, and without that he was lost. He had to imagine how desperation appeared in all its forms, and these were almost infinite. Lost in the labyrinth.

When he had looked for a place for those throwaway papers,

he had wanted a canyon where he could dump the bales without being seen. Now the uneasiness seemed to rise from the pale dirt, since when Farrell had searched for a place to dump papers, he never thought it would come in handy to find a dead girl who had been pushed into the bushes. He understood, with a sweaty rush of claustrophobic anger, what he had lost between then and now.

The Valley didn't look inviting, and the hillsides didn't either. The brush at this time of the year was brown, and the eucalyptus trees made the landscape appear like the African savannah or the Australian outback, at once familiar and still foreign. The sky had a profound indifference. The Universal back lot, which was down below, made Farrell uneasy, since it could be molded into appearing like anything, the steppes of Asia, the plains of Africa, or anything else. The sets were built to appear like a backstreet in Paris, Rome, Prague, or any place at all. Nothing definite in that piece of land: just the possibility of a million illusions.

The pullout at the side of the road was along the top of a slope too steep to build on, and Farrell walked along the brush and kept his eyes on the soft shoulder, just beyond the blacktop. Had anything been dragged across it? Did Terry have the presence of mind to brush out any track? In the middle of the night and high as a weather balloon, Terry wouldn't stop to worry about leaving tracks. Farrell's shoes went around the fast-food wrappers, beer cans, glassine envelopes, and small squares of paper that looked like origami but were the small sheets that had been folded into cocaine bindles. The creases looked like a piece of newspaper that had been folded into a kid's hat. Empty now, left along with the other junk.

An animal had left footprints in the dust. Not that large, probably a medium size dog? Something like that. Of course, Farrell knew someone could bring a dog up here to let it run around and not have to clean up after it. That could explain it. The difficulty was that everything people did left marks, tracks, signs. But it was hard to pick out one that meant something beyond just clutter.

Another possibility presented itself. This search might not turn up what Terry had left, but something else. Something that other people had to hide, or someone to hide, and so there was a possibility of finding, say, the dead husband of a woman who had decided to cash in on his life insurance and had given him a hot shot of insulin and pushed the body into the brush up here.

If something like that was around, what could be done? Call the cops? Farrell didn't think so. What was he doing looking around in the brush? Well, ah, I was just. . . . No. He couldn't say a word. And this realization, no matter what or who had been found, that he wouldn't say a thing, only added to the sense of being in some downward suction. As though what was in the air was in the landscape, the soil, too, and that it exercised a gravitation that worked against what everyone knew was the right thing to do. As the reddish mist thickened, he realized the essential fact of being alone. He considered Catherine, and he imagined talking to her, or saying, "I'd like to ask you something. What do you do when you're feeling alone?"

"Why, nothing," she'd say. "You wait."

"You mean, you pick your chances?"

"Yeah," she'd said. "If you can."

"And the right thing is vengeance?"

The dog tracks went into the brush, which had to be pushed out of the way. Nothing sounds like that buzz of a rattlesnake, sort of similar to a toaster on the fritz. Or some timer that is meant to wake you from the deepest sleep. Sometimes, after pulling the brush one way and then another, after spreading it, the branches snapped into his face. The slight trickle of blood was like an ant crawling on his cheek or the side of his face, and when he wiped it away and then put his finger in his mouth, the sea-like taste of blood lingered. The taste fit the brush, the dust, the valley in the distance.

The silence was of a particular variety, not of malice, but of indifference. No animal was here, just that hiss or that emptiness after the last drops of water flow out of a pitcher. To Farrell this keen lack of sound had a visual element, like a clear piece of plastic that covered everything. Or maybe it had a slight, reddish tint.

He faced the tracks of dogs, coyote, fox, or something else. Who knew what species were moving into the hills?

He looked around where the tracks disappeared into nothing, then moved through the brush back toward the road, got into his car, went another hundred yards, pulled over, and examined the yellow brownish dirt of the shoulder.

11

AFTER THE DUST OF THE canyons, the shoulder of the road, the streets that went toward the Valley from Mulholland, after Farrell sat in his car and listened to the ticking of the engine as it cooled, he went into the house and took a bath. The tub was upstairs, a deep one like those in Japan, where you sat with the water up to your neck. It had a shape more like a refrigerator than a tub. He waited as though the water had some clue, some hint, some suggestion, but Farrell knew this was delusion and superstition. Superstition is the poor man's religion.

Then he made pasta puttanesca, named for whores in Rome who prepared it for their regular clients as a post-trick snack. Anchovies, oil, garlic, black olives, parsley. Puttanesca. The whore's dinner. Who says, thought Farrell, that the unconscious doesn't do its work?

What was he doing? He shook his head, went to the bookshelf, and took down a hardback edition, the dust jacket a little torn at the top and bottom, since the book had been read so often. It fell open to the right place, the page he was looking for. Just a fragment, "That wild longing for clarity . . ."

He put the book and sat down, head in his hands.

That wild longing for clarity. . . .

After midnight, the air was the temperature of human skin, and the warmth had the same smoothness. Indian summer in California is a few weeks of exquisite pleasantness, as though the climate had the perfume of sweet peas. The scent from the hedge, from the roses was mixed with the whiff of the hillside, the brush, and the pleasant scent of the earth and warm pavement.

Farrell's footsteps on the gravel path in front Rose Marie's house made a sound like walking on crushed ice. Her door was unlocked, but as he touched it, pushed against it, he guessed she had a reason for leaving it unlocked.

Rose Marie said, "I'm in the living room."

She sat on her leather sofa, and on the wall behind her she'd hung a quilt with a red and white geometric pattern. The effect was at once cheerful and precise. Rose Marie had a bottle of vodka on the cardboard box she was using for a table. Some ice, too, and two glasses. She poured the water-colored liquor into two glasses and sat there, not drinking, just staring at Farrell. Her hair was pulled back into a ponytail, and the slight freckles showed on her nose. Her fingers were shaking when she reached for her glass, although she kept her eyes on Farrell's.

"Why are you here?" she said. "I didn't ask you to come."

Something lingered in the air, a charge, as when humid air and heat let you know that a flash of electricity is just about to reveal itself.

"Now that you're here, why don't you sit down?"

He sat down next to her. Her scent, from her hair and skin, was a mixture of the ocean and something else, that dark scent of the hillside. She turned her gray eyes on him. Then she tried to reach for her glass again but couldn't do it. She blinked and looked away.

She said, "I didn't ask you . . . I didn't . . ."

He tried not to move.

"Goddamn you," she said. "You piece of shit, you fucking idiot."

She put her face next to his, the texture of her lips so close that the lines were obvious.

"Fuck," she said. "Fuck you."

She leaned closer. Her blouse was a sleeveless one, and when she raised her arm, as though to hit him, there was a slight shadow there where she hadn't shaved. She started crying, leaning across him as though to embrace him, when she did the stubble of the underarm ran like an electric thrill against his lips. She turned back to her glass on the cardboard box, but still she couldn't pick it up with her trembling fingers. Instead, she ripped his shirt open, the buttons flying through the air like bits from an explosion.

"Which one was it?" he said.

She had been alone with the effect of the children and she had gotten used to it, as though it was a shield, and now much to her dismay, her previously unacknowledged loneliness revealed itself in a complexity she hadn't ever imagined, haziness filled with desire, and with a suddenly apparent need for someone else. In the moment, she didn't have time to consider the desire mixed with need and with an intensity that left her trembling. She was left in a new circumstance, which was an awareness of how much vitality she had taken from the children, and when it was gone, she was desperate for a replacement, or a quality that soothed her as she trembled with the effect of death and desire. And the opportunity that came from the sudden appearance, out of nowhere, of the man who sat next to her.

Her palm made a loud slap on his cheek and he tasted blood, the same as when he had scratched himself looking for the British girl and had tasted the blood on his fingers. Rose Marie leaned forward, her scent, her smooth skin, the crush of a breast against him, the ripping sound as she tore at her jeans. Smooth skin, her heaving against him, and her breath on his cheek as she said, "So, so . . . ?" She took his hand

and they went upstairs to her bed, which wasn't made and had the scent of her sleep on the sheets, and there, as she ripped her underwear, her sheer panties, she pulled him down and said, here, here, here, don't move, just stay, just comfort, comfort. The scent of the ocean, or the hillside, the roses all seem to linger in the room, and the rustle of the sheets blended with the gravelly rush of an occasional car as it went up the canyon. Out the window, above the hillside, the red glow of the city lingered, and even then, the light of an occasional star penetrated the mist. As the warm air outside cooled, the first hint of fog began to appear, and then she started to cry again, pulling him closer.

She said, "Just stay here for a while. Don't say a word. Not a word. Or, I will kill you."

The sound, or the hush of the hillside, a wild dog or coyote or something moved in the undergrowth, and then another car came along, the dust from the road filling the air and making a cloud of bright points in the headlights of the car that followed. So, they just waited, breathing, feeling the damp places get cold.

"It happens so fast with the kids," she said.

"Which one?" he said.

"Oh, shit," she said.

"A favorite?" he said.

"They are all favorites," she said.

"Catherine?" he said.

"No," said Rose Marie. "It wasn't Catherine. It was a girl too sick to come to meet you. But I don't think Catherine has too much time. Either."

"What was the girl's name?"

"Janey," she said. "The girl just vanished . . . just like that."

Rose Marie put her hand on Farrell's face, then went downstairs to the kitchen for ice, which she brought in a cloth napkin. The ice in a napkin felt cool on his cheek.

She said, "I didn't hurt you, did I? I was just so . . ."

She pushed the napkin harder against his cheek.

"It doesn't matter," he said.

"More rough trade, huh?" she said.

"No," he said. "It just doesn't matter."

"Don't you dare say you are sorry," she said. "About my kid. About Janey."

Rose Marie glanced down as she trembled.

"By the way," she said, when she glanced up again, "Catherine really likes you. She sent me a text. I think she even has a crush on you."

"She's lovely," he said. "She'd grow into a lovely woman."

"Yes," she said. "And you know what? She knows I have a crush on you, too." Rose Marie swallowed.

"I'm sorry I was like that," she said. "That I slapped you."

"It takes more than that to hurt me," he said.

She scrambled some eggs and they sat at her kitchen table and ate them, not saying a word. Then she was able to have a drink and looked at him.

"Catherine wants you to do the right thing. I do, too."

"I know," he said. "I'm working on it."

"The kids really liked you. And they want to know about Terry Peregrine."

"He's weak and scared," he said. "That's the most dangerous man there is."

"They don't have to know that, do they?"

He shrugged.

"Just let me stay for a while," he said. "So, I can think things over."

"I'm going to take a shower," she said.

"No," he said. "No. Just lie down with me. Let's go back upstairs."

"Catherine may die soon. Will die soon. That's all she's got left, the hope of someone keeping that promise ..."

"Upstairs," he said. "Leave the window open so we can smell the hillside."

"Yes," said Rose Marie. "Indian summer doesn't last."

12

THE PEOPLE FARRELL HELPED LIVED on the coast, not in Malibu itself, but off the roads to the right, to the east, if you were going north on the Pacific Coast Highway. Others lived little farther north, even as far as some towns inland from Santa Barbara. An easy commute for actors and other people who got into trouble.

This meant donations to police department benevolent funds, and more direct contributions, always in used bills, always in an envelope that was generic, just something he would pass along to a coroner, or a head of detectives in a town where he needed help. Farrell had done this in every town and jurisdiction from Long Beach to Santa Ynez. Records, details, arrests. People were always glad to see him. Who doesn't want to see money coming in the door?

Portia and Charlene lived in Santa Monica. Jerry Macaulay, who worked the Juvenile Section of the Santa Monica Police Department, said when Farrell called, "Hey, Farrell, where you been. I miss hearing from you. Keeping your nose clean?" Macaulay spoke as though he was explaining to a teller at the bank that his daughter was having her teeth straightened.

"As much as can be expected," said Farrell. "Could you give me what you have on Portia Blanchard and Charlene Klauski. That's K-l-a-u-s-k-i. They live in Santa Monica."

"Hang on," said Macaulay.

Farrell held the phone to his ear, breathed deeply to get the scent of the roses, and while he waited, he opened the front door. He glanced at Rose Marie's house. Maybe she was making the bed with a snap of the top sheet, like a flag in the wind. . . .

"Well, well," said Macaulay. "It could be better but it could be worse. They didn't try to kill anyone, but they have records for suspected prostitution, attempted blackmail, shoplifting, making false statements about being raped, and, of course, some drug possession. Coke. The usual. Blanchard's mother, by the way, that's Cherry Blanchard, has an arrest for prostitution."

"Thanks," said Farrell. "I know how expenses add up. One thing and another."

"Thanks, pal," said Macaulay.

The JennAir refrigerator in his kitchen made a low, ominous hum. Farrell lingered in the domestic air of the toast and coffee.

If you are going to deal with the cops, maybe it is best to do it all at once and get it over with. He winced, shrugged, and picked up the phone.

He wasn't surprised that Shirushi kept tabs on him, or the people he gave money to, and, sure, he thought, she was right about Tommy Black. Still, since cops were gossiping anyway, maybe it was best to see them all as fast as possible. Let them think they knew what he was doing.

Of course he was ready to cause some trouble, but to do that he had to know what was real, and in a place like LA that wasn't easy.

He had set a Google News Alert for sex crimes in Los Angeles, and he learned that James Karicek, twenty-four years old, featured in the *Los Angeles Times*, the man who had mesmerized Terry, and who had been accused of drugging and sleeping with underage girls and the occasional boy, had been released on bail.

"Hey, Farrell," said Tommy Black. "Long time since I heard from you. Everybody must be behaving themselves."

"Can I come down to see you?" he said.

"Sure," said Tommy. "Always good to talk face-to-face."

Santa Monica Boulevard, in Hollywood, was a collection of hairdressers, dry cleaners, coffee shops, florists, insurance offices, all arranged in a sort of insane clutter, an expression of chaos. Farrell didn't know whether it was his mood or the actual businesses that left him with the notion that it made no sense at all.

The Barnum & Bailey Circus had a tradition, when Farrell had been a kid, of parading the elephants down Santa Monica Boulevard at 4:00 a.m. . . . Nothing, it seemed, was as sad as a circus. One step down from a zoo.

Tommy's office building looked like a post office, as though crime was more bureaucratic than anything else. And, when Farrell thought about it, this seemed right. Dull. Tommy Black's desk was an institutional item that looked like it had been made with a 3D printer. A block of gray plastic.

"So, how can I help today?" Tommy Black said.

"Are you still working the sex crimes detail for beach cities?"

"Some things never change," said Tommy.

"Are your kids doing all right? Do they need braces?"

"No," said Tommy. "But there's always something."

"I understand," Farrell said.

"Good," said Tommy. "What's on your mind?"

"I wouldn't go so far as to say everyone is behaving themselves."

"Well, just how far would you go?" said Black.

"It depends," he said. "I'll recognize it when I see it."

"Well, yeah," said Tommy. "What can you expect? Human beings, for Chrissake."

"That's the problem?" Farrell said. "Being human?"

"I don't think about stuff like that," said Black. "And you know what? If I were you, I wouldn't either. Just do your job. Hope you get out alive. That's my philosophy of life."

"Sure," Farrell said. "Are you still running the home detention section?"

"Let's go out in the hall," said Tommy. "Out by the vending machines. Better to talk there. You bought into vending machines, right? Don't you have a little business on the side? No trouble with shakedowns?"

"Not yet," Farrell said.

"Wait for a while," said Tommy Black. "Vending machines are like a dog in heat for the shakedown artists. What's it called?"

"Coin-A-Matic," Farrell said. "You wouldn't believe the stuff people put into vending machines, slugs, flattened bottle caps, all to get a free Mars Bar, or a bag of chips. And then we got another problem. Rodents."

"Rodents?" said Tommy. "You're telling me about rodents?" He hiked up his pants. "Do you think technology is going to put Coin-A-Matic out of business?"

"No," Farrell said. "We'll just get better machines. You know, they have one that makes hot, fresh pizza. You can choose the toppings and the thing cooks the pizza right there. In the bus station or hall of the probation office."

"No shit," said Tommy. "I'd like to get one here."

"So, it's Gino's and the chain pizza places that are going to be in trouble."

"All right," said Tommy. "Make it fast. What's on your mind?"

"Karicek," Farrell said.

"Karicek," said Tommy. "A real hall of famer. What a guy. You'd think he'd learn to leave girls under sixteen alone. Wouldn't you?"

"You could hope," Farrell said.

"Define hope," said Black.

"Some other time," said Farrell. "You let Karicek out night before last. Where is he?"

"Let me look it up," said Tommy.

Tommy Black went into his office, the rubber soles of his shoes squeaking on the linoleum, which was like an eternal sound of police offices. Farrell looked at the vending machine, which had some wrinkled looking bags of chips and chocolate chip cookies. Desperation food. The click of computer keys came into the hall, then Tommy Black's voice as he mumbled greetings to someone on a phone. . . . More steps on the linoleum. In the hall, Tommy said, "Manhattan Beach. The Brooklyn Bridge motel. Jesus, you'd think they'd be able to think of something better than that. Manhattan. Brooklyn. Get it?"

"Yeah," said Farrell.

"We got a judge here that just loves to turn 'em loose," said Tommy.

It wouldn't do me much good if he was in jail, thought Farrell.

"I'll buy you a drink soon," said Farrell.

"I'd like that," said Tommy. "Just make sure you remember your friends, right?"

Friends.

"Thanks, Tommy," he said. "I'll be in touch."

"I'll be waiting," said Tommy.

* * *

Farrell got lucky. The movie crew was shooting a scene in which only other actors were needed. Terry had a day off. After Tommy Black, Farrell was able to call Terry to make sure that the girls and Cherry Blanchard would be at Terry's house in the afternoon.

Farrell came into the living room. The time the girls and Cherry had waited hadn't done them any good. Portia had that look of anger that comes from the third or the fourth argument, and Charlene sulked under Portia's gaze. Cherry wore a khaki skirt, a blue blouse, had her hair in a ponytail, and wore shoes with a low heel, as though she could compensate for the mood here with a hint of modesty. Terry wore jeans, a Biarritz T-shirt, a pair of running shoes without socks.

"So, we've almost got this worked out, right?" Terry said to Farrell.

Terry's expression, his presence, had a quality so false, so oddly insincere it was as though he didn't exist at all, and that emptiness was the quality that Farrell watched. What was there in that vacuum? Wasn't that the problem Farrell confronted, that emptiness? No, not just the emptiness, but what it could do.

Cherry sat on the edge of the sofa, her eyes at once angry and worried, hopeful and terrified.

"I'm working on getting you your lines," Farrell said. "The director is being difficult."

"Difficult?" said Portia. "I'll show him difficult."

"I understand," Farrell said.

"Do you?" she said. "Somehow you aren't acting like it. And you know what? I am getting impatient."

Cherry smiled at Farrell as though to say, You know how kids are.

Portia was too angry for just putting the bite on someone.

"The other night, when Terry took the British girl to the doctor," said Farrell. "How long was he gone?"

"Why are you harping on that?" said Terry. "That's all gone. Done with."

"Portia?" said Farrell.

"I don't know," she said, as she looked out the window. "Ten minutes, an hour. We were all pretty messed up."

"Forget it," said Terry. "Let's fix our problems right here."

"Yeah," said Portia to Terry. "Can't you call the director? To speed things up. To get really good lines."

"I can't talk to him about this," said Terry. "He'll want to know why."

"Tell him you have found some talented young actresses who are a tremendous asset ..."

"Well, you know, he's heard things like that before . . . . not to mention a producer is involved, too."

"I keep telling you," said Portia. "That's not my problem."

"We want the lines," said Charlene. "It's a start. A credit. Our names on a card."

"They are talented," said Cherry. "They deserve a chance. So, they slept with you, but that doesn't take away from their talent."

"They were pretty talented," said Terry.

"That's not what I meant," said Cherry. "You have to do the right thing."

Farrell put five thousand dollars, in dirty bills, on the table now. The glass was scratched from the use of a razor blade.

"What's that?" said Terry.

"Good faith," said Farrell. "Just to buy a little time."

Portia poked at the money. Charlene stared. They looked at each other. Were they going to take it or not?

"I'm sorry about the lines," said Terry.

"Not as sorry as I am," said Portia. Then she turned that gaze on Farrell.

"If I were you, I'd take the money and let's see what happens," said Farrell.

Terry's glance had the cool, estimating quality of a falcon as it circles in the air. Yes, thought Farrell, Catherine had been right. Look out for birds of prey as they circle.

Portia stared, those dark, artificial eyes drilling into Farrell. That was another item he hadn't seen before, a hatred without limit. Usually it was disappointment or regret, but here it was fury so strong it had a stink.

"So, you think we're just kids you can push around. Don't you?" said Portia. "You better think again."

"Charlene?" Farrell said. "What about you?"

"Portia's gonna talk for us," said Charlene.

"Good."

"We could still go to the cops," said Portia.

"We've been through that," said Farrell.

He picked up the money and put it in the pocket of his jacket.

"Go the cops. It's the end," he said to Portia. "And I think they'll pull up a couple of things. Like your record."

"What about my record?" said Portia.

"She's a good girl," said Cherry. "Never any trouble."

Her face was blank, like a bank teller who is at the end of the day and needs a drink. Farrell was sorry for her and wished he could stop what was coming.

"Suspicion of prostitution," he said. "Possession of drugs. Making false statements to a police officer, which really was an attempt at blackmail over a false accusation of rape."

"That's just, you know, semantics," said Cherry.

Charlene looked at her shoes.

"And me?" she said. "My record?"

"Yeah," Farrell said. "You, too."

"And so what do you want?" said Portia.

"A little time," said Farrell. "That's all. Just some time."

"And you'll leave the money," said Portia. "As good faith."

Farrell put the money on the table.

"Okay, Mr. Jones," said Portia. "You bought a little time. But not much."

13

As he drove back to Laurel Canyon, the caller ID showed Shirushi. Fast work, thought Farrell.

"Hey, Farrell," she said. "I've got something for you."

The car had been in the sunlight in front of Terry's house, and now it felt like he was sitting on a heating pad.

"So?" said Farrell.

"Let's meet," said Shirushi.

"I've got things to do," said Farrell. "Just tell me."

"I want to see your face," said Shirushi. "Let's meet in Studio City. That sounds about right."

Du-par's was the closest thing in the Valley or Los Angeles for that matter to a Parisian boulangerie. On the right, near the door, stood a long glass case in which there were cream puffs, cakes, cookies, and the overall impression was a line of tarts made from bright fruit, strawberries, raspberries, cherries, and all of them were topped with white, cloud-like whipped cream.

Shirushi sat in a booth when Farrell arrived, a cream puff and a cup of coffee on the table in front of her. Dark eyes on him as he came in, still wearing his uniform of the invisible outfitter. He sat down and the waitress brought him a cup of coffee.

Cream leaked out of the pastry when Shirushi cut into it, and she licked the fork she put into her mouth. A little of the white fluff clung to her lip, and she ran her tongue over it.

"Mmmmm," she said. "I've always had a sweet tooth. Don't know why. Now, I'll have to swim an extra mile at my pool tonight. Worth it though. Want a bite?"

She held out a fork with some cream and pastry.

"Thanks," said Farrell. "Some other time. So?"

She swallowed and looked at him as though she was working out a trigonometric proof.

"So, what do you know about Terry Peregrine?" she said.

Farrell shook his head.

"Is that, no, you don't know anything, or no, you can't tell me anything?"

"What did you find out?" said Farrell.

"They're brothers. Karicek and Peregrine. Same mother. She, by the way, is in the women's prison in Alderson, West Virginia. Murder. A boyfriend, of course, but he was selling young women to a pimp in New York City."

She went back to her cream puff. Then she glanced at Farrell.

"So?" she said.

Farrell shrugged, as though he had a pain in his shoulder, then winced and said, "I don't know. That's about all I can say."

"You look like you've got a headache," she said. "You want an aspirin?"

"No, I don't want an a-a-aspirin," he said.

"Just asking," she said. "You don't have to get huffy."

"I'm not huffy," he said.

"Define what you are," she said.

"Give me a break," he said.

"Sure, sure," she said. "I get it. I give you information and you blow me off. Sure. That's right."

She finished her cream puff. Licked the fork.

"I don't know much," she said. "But something like this, that Terry's brother has been caught with underage women, can do a lot of damage to someone in the movie business."

Farrell looked right at her.

"That's right," he said.

"So, right now," she said. "I should be careful. I don't know anything, but I could start looking."

Farrell looked at his cup of coffee and at that black circle of the surface.

"How did you think there was something between them?" said Shirushi.

"Family resemblance," said Farrell.

"Have you seen Terry Peregrine recently?" she said.

"Don't, don't . . ." he said. "Just don't . . ."

"Well, no one has made any complaint," she said. "I have no reason to dig into any of this. Now."

"Then wait a little," he said.

"So, you want me to put this in the secrets category?" she said.

"That's right," he said.

She stared at him and said, "I'll think about it."

"Okay," he said. "Do you want another cream puff?"

"No," she said. "I've had enough. Take care." She picked up the check. "My treat."

Shirushi put a twenty-dollar bill on the table. When the waitress brought the change, Shirushi left it. The waitress said, "Thanks, honey."

"Remember," said Shirushi to Farrell. "What I said about getting left holding the bag."

* * *

In the silence of Farrell's house, which was on the other side of the hill from Du-par's, he knew, without any doubt, that Shirushi wouldn't wait too long. She was certain, like any good cop, that something was wrong. The question for her was just what it could be. And, for that matter, Farrell wasn't even sure he knew himself, although he surely was going to find out.

He was alarmed by the sluggishness of his thinking and the sudden moment when it was obvious how wrong he had been in the way he had searched. It was evening and the front yard of Farrell's house was dusky. Only one dim light was on in Rose Marie's house, but she was there, and just that faint glow, that domestic haze from the window, left him with an ache. Then he checked his voice mail.

Braumberg wanting to know "how things were." Bob Marshall said that that Pavel and Nikolay had come by to "try to scare me." It sounded to Farrell like they had done a pretty good job of that.

Farrell called Marshall back and said, "Too bad I missed them."

"*Too bad?*" Marshall said. "*Too bad?* That's just great."

He was equally angry at Farrell and the Russians.

"We got another problem," Marshall said. "A raccoon has gotten into a vending machine in a mini-mart on Ventura. It won't come out, even when I told the Indian guy who runs the place to leave the back panel off. The raccoon just sits in there and it's drooling, too. People try to buy Cheez-Its, but the raccoon charges at them from behind the glass." He waited. "We could call the animal control people."

"No," Farrell said. "We don't want anybody poking around in our machines . . ."

"But Adrith . . ."

"The Indian guy?" Farrell said.

"Yeah. He's bugging out."

"We'll pick up the machine and bring it to the shop."

"I've got news for you," Marshall said. "Adrith has already done that. He's put the machine, a USI Mercato 500, on a dolly, brought it over here, and left it. Right here. The raccoon is right in there, moving around."

"Okay," Farrell said. "All right."

The light switches in Farrell's house were a small, odd comfort, since he knew where they were in the dusk. The light came like a small blessing and the refrigerator hummed. The ice maker dropped a load of clinking cubes into the box in the freezer.

Then Rose Marie made the hinges of the door squeak as she came in, and when she sat down opposite Farrell, she said, "Uh-oh."

Farrell shrugged.

"Hey," said Rose Marie. "It's like the joke about the horse that goes into a bar."

"Yeah?" he said.

"Yeah," said Rose Marie. "The bartender says, 'Why the long face?'"

"Do you think it's the horse's fault?"

"Of course not. That's the joke," said Rose Marie.

He put two small glasses, like those in Paris cafés, on the table, one for Rose Marie and one for himself. Then he took a bottle of calvados from the cupboard and poured each of them a drink.

"Let's pretend we're in Paris. In the Sixth at a café on Rue de Buci. Just down from the flower market."

"Now there's an idea," she said. "You really are a romantic."

He shrugged.

"There are worse things," he said.

He sat in the slight, faintly sea-like intimation of her skin and hair, then reached over and took her hand.

"You think we are an item?" he said.

"Is that what you think?" she said.

"You know, it's been a long time," he said. "But, if you want to know the truth, I think we are."

"Just like that?" she said.

"Yeah," he said. "It can happen fast."

"Sort of makes my head spin," she said.

Farrell's phone lit up. The caller ID showed Coin-A-Matic.

"Answer it," she said.

"All right, Bob," he said into the phone. "This isn't the best time."

"You better come now . . ." Marshall said.

"You just called," Farrell said.

"One more thing like this and I quit," he said. "You know what I'm saying?"

Farrell glanced at Rose Marie and said, "He wants to know when I'm going to come down there to help him out? You know, Bob Marshall. The guy who works for me. In this business I bought. What an idea that turned out to be."

Rose Marie sat next to him and whispered in his ear, the warm, moist breath seeming to go right through him.

"You know what the difference between a husband and a lover is?"

"No, what?"

"About twenty minutes," she said.

"I'll leave here in about an hour," Farrell said to Bob. "Will that do it?"

"The animal is running around in there. Do you think the thing inside is rabid?" said Bob. "You know I don't want to get bitten."

"I'll leave in an hour," Farrell said.

"Very smooth," said Rose Marie. "Come on. Let's go upstairs. Then I want to go with you to see this place. The tax dodge."

"Who said anything about a tax dodge?" he said.

She raised an eyebrow.

"Okay," he said. "You can come. Do you speak Russian?"

"What's that supposed to mean?" she said.

She put her lips against him, just a brushing touch.

"So, you're determined to get rid of the long face?" he said.

"That's right," said Rose Marie.

They sat together and let the warmth build where they touched, along the thighs and hip. Just quiet, which had its own language, if one can say that, a way of speaking to one another.

"Don't worry," he said. "I'm coming to see your kids again."

"Ah," she said. "With a little encouragement I could fall in love with you."

Oh, he thought. If you only could.

14

THE SIGN FOR COIN-A-MATIC WAS in a wedding invitation script on a white background, as though vending machines could be gussied up by a traditional font. The large doors of the building, with a small door inside one of them, suggested that if you went in, you were getting into more than you bargained for. Rose Marie sat with the seat belt across her chest, her hair a little ruffled, her skin a little abrased. She glanced at Farrell and said, "Maybe I was wrong. Maybe I should have said the difference between a lover and a husband is forty-five minutes."

"But we're just getting started," Farrell said.

"So it will be sort of like a bedroom bake-off," she said.

She smiled with such a lascivious grin he was left blinking and wondering what he had got himself into.

"So, this is it?" she said. She gestured to the door of the Coin-A-Matic.

"This is it," he said. "Do you know much about raccoons?"

"Not really," she said.

"I can tell you this," he said. "They seem to like Cheez-Its and Milk Duds . . ."

"So, you have one in a machine?" she said.

"That's about the size of it . . ."

"You look worried," she said. "It's just a raccoon . . ."

"Well, I'm not so worried about the animal," he said.

There's the British girl for one, and another matter. Mary Jones. What happened the night she was there, at Terry's place?

"Penny for your thoughts," said Rose Marie.

"Oh, I don't know," he said.

"Slippery," she said.

Inside the warehouse, not far from the open door, they approached the machine. It was still strapped to the dolly. Bob Marshall was pacing in front of it. If you looked closely and could imagine Bob twenty-five pounds lighter and with a little more hair, you could see the child actor he had been on *San Pedro Blues*. The show he was on was about a fisherman and they had adventures every week, fish pirates, smugglers, lovers who weren't getting along. Marshall had been a heavy kid, and his role was to look confused at what was happening with, say, the fish pirates, and at the end of the show he was a little wiser than before. Then he had lost the leg on a British motorcycle he kept on Catalina, a Panther Cat, the injury suggesting, as Farrell thought, the darkness the TV show had hinted at but always escaped. Now, Marshall limped on that leg, with his socks held up by thumbtacks, his eyes on Farrell, then on Rose Marie.

"Rose Marie," Farrell said. "This is Bob Marshall."

"Not *the* Bob Marshall," she said. "From *San Pedro Blues*?"

"In the flesh," he said.

"When I was a kid, I watched that show all the time," said Rose Marie. "What happened?"

Bob pulled up his blue jeans to show his leg, and the white socks held up with the red thumbtack.

"Motorcycle," he said. "Pretty cool with the thumbtacks, huh?"

"Sure," said Rose Marie, who, after all, had seen everything. Or just about. Or had had enough surprises to last a lifetime.

"Yeah," he said. "It's like a bulletin board. One day I'm going to leave a note, tacked to my leg for him."

He pointed to Farrell.

"Let's get these straps off the machine," said Farrell.

"I don't know," said Bob. "The animal gets stirred up pretty easy."

It was an old-style machine with large, wire screws that held the chips, the orange crackers with peanut butter, and the Twizzlers.

"You can do it," said Bob. "If you want to get the straps off."

At the first couple of clicks of the ratchet, the animal rushed to the window in front of the crackers and the candy bars in their festive wrappings. It hissed, scratched at the glass, slobbered, weaved from side to side, and while it was doing that it kept its eyes on Farrell. It had a mask just like a robber.

"I didn't know a raccoon hissed," said Rose Marie.

"Let me tell you," said Bob. "They can growl, hiss, make a sound like a dog. Gives you a moment's pause. You know, you don't want to reach in there."

"Especially if it's rabid," Farrell said.

"That's what I'm saying," said Bob.

"It won't go out the back panel?"

"Take a look," he said.

"I've heard that raccoons like sardines," said Rose Marie.

"How do you know that?" said Bob.

"A kid I knew told me," said Rose Marie.

"Must have lived in the hills out toward Malibu," said Bob. "Is that where she lived?"

"At one time. Then she had to move," said Rose Marie.

"Where to?"

"Westwood," she said.

"Westwood?" he said. "Down toward UCLA? No raccoons down there, I bet."

Rose Marie swallowed.

"Well, yeah," said Bob. "I guess. Out there in Malibu they are building houses like nobody's business. You know what the real estate developers think?"

"Tell me," said Rose Marie.

"They look at a piece of land and they think, Yeah, it's a beautiful place to build a house, and yeah, it's gonna burn. But guess what? When it does, someone else is going to own it."

"Give me a broom, will you?" Farrell said to Bob.

"I wouldn't do that, if I were you," said Bob.

Farrell undid the straps, backed the dolly away, and left the machine on the concrete of the floor. Behind it were the cardboard cases of crackers, chips, Mars Bars, Twizzlers, and next to it stood a workbench with its screwdrivers, socket wrenches, a soldering iron, a vise, a hacksaw, and some small fuses that the newer, electronic machines used. A couple of small motherboards.

With the back panel off there was an opening about two feet by three, the darkness filled with a musty, animal scent. Bob handed Farrell the broom.

"I don't want to be a party pooper but rabies is a very serious disease," said Rose Marie. "If you don't get the shots, you know that the mortality rate is close to 90 percent?"

"No kidding," said Bob.

"So, if I can get it to come out of there, then you should stand back," Farrell said.

The animal scratched the metal surface inside as it moved back and forth.

"I'll whack on the glass and chase him toward the back, where you are," Farrell said. "Oh, shit. Wait. He's just taken a peanut butter cracker. I'll hit the front of it."

The sound was like a bum trying to get a free bag of chips by banging on the machine, and then the raccoon threw itself against the glass of the front and turned and ran toward the back.

Rose Marie said, "Look out. Here he comes."

The raccoon appeared at the open panel, its eyes on Farrell's, still with that accusatory quality, which made him think of the brush along the side of Mulholland Drive. He moved the broom to the side to get it behind the animal in the machine. The raccoon took a step back and hissed. The details of Farrell's worries lingered like an old habit, or a recurrent mood. Were there raccoons off Mulholland?

"By the way," Farrell aid to Bob. "You haven't gotten the money out of here yet, have you?"

"Are you kidding?"

"Okay," Farrell said. "How much so you think is in there?"

"Got to be five hundred. Reach in there and get the money," said Bob.

"So, you won't reach in there but you think I should?" said Farrell.

"You're the boss," said Bob.

The raccoon grabbed the brushy end of the broom, and when Farrell tried to drag it out, the creature pulled back, and Farrell had sensation that he wasn't pulling it out, but that the animal was pulling him in. Its dark eyes, in that moment, made Farrell think of the British girl with the Goth tattoo.

"What are you doing?" said a man with a Russian accent. This was Pavel, who had bad acne scars. Maybe that's what the KGB looked for in its recruits, someone with bad skin. He had short, regular teeth, although one of them was gold.

"We were just passing by and saw the light. We figured that you must be counting the take, right?" said Nikolay.

"Look at that," Pavel said to Nikolay. "It's an *yenot* . . . right inside that machine."

"I didn't think they had them here," said Nikolay. "I thought they were in the Caucus or in Siberia . . ."

"Yeah, Siberia," said Pavel with a wistfulness. . . .

"What's the broom for?" said Nikolay.

"He's trying to chase the *yenot* out of the machine . . ." said Pavel.

"Might work," said Nikolay.

"Who is this?" said Pavel. He lifted his chin toward Rose Marie and at the logo for the Children's Hospital on the T-shirt she wore. "And what's that hospital?"

"It's where I work," she said.

"Huh," said Nikolay. "We had a lot of sick kids after Chernobyl. Thyroid tumors, leukemia . . ."

"We see a lot of leukemia . . ." said Rose Marie.

"Yeah, I guess," said Pavel. He turned to Farrell and said, "Well, you know why we're here."

"Yeah," he said.

"It's five hundred now," said Pavel. "So, forget the *yenot* and get us the money."

Rose Marie shifted her weight from one leg to another, and then glanced at Farrell.

"Well, I've got news for you," Farrell said.

"What's that?" said Pavel. He put his hands on his hips.

"Your money," he said. He pointed to the back of the machine, above the dark opening. "Is in there."

"Hmm," said Pavel.

"Are you afraid to reach in there?" said Bob.

"Are you calling me a coward?" said Pavel.

"I'm saying your money is right in there and why don't you just pick it up and get out of here."

Bob really had been a good actor. He moved a little closer to Pavel.

Farrell pushed the broom back in. The raccoon hissed, and then made a hoot that was so much like an owl that a pigeon, visible on the street through the open door at the front of the building, flew away.

"You're just scaring it," said Pavel.

"Well, reach in to get the money," said Bob.

"What did you say?" said Pavel.

"I think we should all take a big deep breath," said Rose Marie. Her forehead was damp now, and her eyes seemed a little larger than usual. She stepped back, hugging herself.

"I'm breathing just fine," said Nikolay. Then he turned to Bob and said, "You're still calling me a coward, aren't you?"

"I'm saying there is your money," said Bob.

"Take it easy, Bob," Farrell said. "Rose Marie is right. Let's just calm down and figure out how we are going to take care of this."

"Too late for that," said Pavel.

The raccoon ran from side to side, scratching, moving around among the peanut butter crackers, the chips, the candy bars. It kept turning its eyes on Farrell.

"You aren't trying to scare me, are you?" said Bob.

"I want you to reach in there and to get the money and to give it to me," said Pavel.

"Get lost," said Bob.

Farrell shook his head, No, no, no. . . .

Pavel reached under his arm, took out a .38 Police Special, short nosed, a revolver. He pulled back the hammer, put it against Bob's leg and pulled the trigger. The noise was so loud that all of them couldn't hear. The bullet went into Bob's blue jeans and came out the other side, where it hit the concrete floor with the sound of a ball-peen hammer. Bob sat back, on the chair behind him, and those years when he had been an actor showed themselves.

"I've been shot," said Bob. "Oh god. It hurts. It runs up to my back. Oh, god."

"Christ," said Nikolay. "Now they are going to call the cops."

"No," said Pavel. He glanced at Farrell. "This guy doesn't want to call the cops."

"No," Farrell said. "I don't think so."

"See," said Pavel.

"Are you going to let this guy bleed to death?" said Nikolay.

"I don't know yet," Pavel said. He turned to Farrell. "So, what are you going to do?"

"Why don't you reach in there and get your money and get out of here," Farrell said.

"You think I won't?" said Pavel.

Having shot someone in the leg had given him a boost. Pavel reached to the back of the machine, put his hand up to the box where the bills landed when someone put a ten or twenty or a five into the machine. The raccoon bit him twice, and then went back into the dark. Pavel yanked his hand out. The web of flesh between his thumb and index finger had glistening red spots that began to bleed.

They stood there while the raccoon went from one side of the machine to the other, slobbering a little now, and seeming to have gotten the same thing out of biting a hand that Pavel had gotten out of shooting someone in the leg. The tension in the room was like the air just before a thunderstorm.

"If it's rabid," said Nikolay. "I've got to have the animal. They test it to see if it's got the disease."

Pavel pointed the pistol at glass of the front of the machine.

"No," Farrell said. "Do you know how much one of these machines costs? No. Don't shoot."

Bob moaned. Really, thought Farrell, it's too bad about the motorcycle and the leg. He *had* been pretty good.

"I'll take care of it," Farrell said.

"Yeah?" said Pavel. "What are we going to do about this?"

He held out the bite on his hand. A number of small marks, as though he had been cut with a saw, each one of them the color of a ruby.

Rose Marie kept her eyes on Farrell's, as though if he could just fix this, she'd know he wasn't another fraud. And where the kids were concerned, the last thing she needed was fraud.

"And what about him?" said Nikolay.

He pointed to Bob.

"All right, Bob," Farrell said. "That's enough."

He pinched Marshall's pant leg, pulled it up, and showed the wooden leg, which had a neat hole in the ash that it was made out of, the same wood that baseball bats were made of.

"Thank god," said Pavel.

"That's the first part," Farrell said.

"What's next?" said Nikolay.

"You wait here for thirty minutes, and I'll fix it," Farrell said.

"My hand is beginning to hurt," said Pavel.

Rose Marie and Farrell went out and got into his car. She was visible in the light of streetlamp, and she trembled and glanced over at Farrell. They drove to Sunset and then up Laurel Canyon.

"You could have asked first," she said. "About Scooter."

"All right," he said. "Can I borrow him for about an hour?"

The hedge in front of the houses was lighted into a golden green, like a movie set. He parked, and then they went into her house, got the glass habitat, and put it in the back seat of the Camry.

"He's hungry," said Rose Marie. "I haven't fed him in a while."

The coils of the creature looked like an enormous inner tube that had been patched with camouflage-colored material. As they adjusted the glass tank, the coils of the python contracted, the movement of them smooth, like something from another world where there were no wheels or gears . . . the pile of it became not smaller but a little higher, and in the background the head rose, and the tongue began to move back and forth.

"You know what he's doing?" said Rose Marie. "With his tongue? He's smelling things."

As they drove, Rose Marie put her hand into the back seat to steady the habitat when they went around a turn, but she kept her eyes straight ahead.

"Maybe you can tell my kids about this," she said.

"That depends," Farrell said. "On how it works out."

She glanced over.

"Maybe I should wait in the car," she said.

"Yes," he said. "Maybe that's a good idea. But you won't."

Her fingers, open like a fan, trembled.

"It will be over soon," he said.

"Is that a promise or a hope?" she said.

Inside the building Nikolay and Pavel stood around the workbench. A paper towel, with a spot of blood on it, was wrapped around Pavel's hand. It was clear that the pain from the bite was throbbing, although he was stoic.

The habitat sat on the floor, the inside of the glass covered with a mist, like a cold drink on a hot day. Farrell guessed that Scooter made the inside cooler, or that the condensation came from his breath. Those green eyes lingered on him, as though it knew precisely who was going to cause trouble.

"What's that?" said Pavel.

"Oh, no," said Nikolay. "It's a *piton* . . ."

"I thought they only had them in Florida or Vietnam or some other hellhole."

"Well, what do you think this place is?" said Nikolay.

The glass cover, like a windowpane, slid off the top of the habitat with a grating noise, not quite like fingernails on a blackboard, but not totally unlike it either. The coils, that pile of a patched inner tube, contracted, and the tongue moved more quickly. It knew something new was around.

"You think it can smell us?" said Nikolay.

The raccoon came to the front glass, beneath the chips, and kept its eyes on the habitat. Farrell had never seen a wild animal look afraid, and it had always been a comfort to him that there are creatures who live without fear, but this seemed to be the exception. The raccoon backed up, into the darkness of the machine.

"Get one of those heavyweight construction trash bags," he said to Bob. "Open it and hold it at the back of the machine."

"Me? Me?" he said.

"Christ," said Rose Marie. "Give it to me."

"No problem. You want to do it, fine by me."

The python's skin wasn't cool, or warm, or anything at all, and if Farrell had to judge by temperature, he'd say the thing was invisible. It was ominous and as Farrell picked it up, it began to wrap itself around his arm, and as it did, the coils moved, not tightening exactly, but not leaving any room for much movement. Of course, that's the way a constrictor works. They don't squeeze anything. They just wrap themselves around a creature and then wait for it to exhale. Then they take up the slack. And in that discomfort with the snake on Farrell's arm, he thought that this is the way, or part of the way, that people like Terry Peregrine worked, moving from trouble to larger trouble, like the girl with the Goth tattoo.

The python put its head at the entrance to the back of the machine, and then with a slow, mesmerizing uncoiling it flowed from his arm, like heavy oil, into the dark opening. The raccoon, in front of the machine, stood absolutely still, as though it was a photograph of itself. Its eyes turned to the back, where the python had begun to flow.

"It knows something is coming," Farrell said.

"Yes," said Rose Marie. She was at the back of the machine but she didn't need to look.

"It's trying to decide whether it should get out or get eaten," said Farrell.

"Just like in Moscow, in the old days," said Pavel.

The raccoon ran to the side of the machine, where the moving, patched coil began to slither into the dark, and then the raccoon made a high-pitched, keening, almost musical cry, like a note that was dying away. It jumped over the coil, its head turned once over its shoulder and then it went, without a moment's hesitation, into the black bag that Rose Marie held at the back panel. She pulled the blue drawstring tight, and with the bag heaving, she passed it over to Pavel, who took the thing, but held it at arm's length.

"When you tell the emergency room doctor that this is the animal that bit you, maybe you should have a story about how you caught it," she said.

The sheet metal box that held the bills was cool to the touch, a lot more cool than the python. Farrell reached in and picked up the bills. Then, on the workbench, next to the socket wrenches and cans of 3-in-One Oil, he counted out five hundred dollars.

"Here," he said.

Nikolay picked it up. Then he glanced at Bob, at Farrell, and Rose Marie, and said, "Where's the closest emergency room?"

"In Westwood," said Rose Marie.

"All right," said Nikolay.

They stood next to the machine, Pavel glancing down at the hole in the pant leg of Bob's jeans, and then at Farrell.

"Good luck getting the *piton* out of there . . ." said Pavel.

"You want me to shoot it?" said Nikolay.

"No," said Rose Marie.

Nikolay shrugged, and then they walked outside, where the moths were moving around the flood lamp like snowflakes in a storm. The Russians looked back, their faces having the same expression of someone who has been close to being run down by a freight train, but who somehow, through means they didn't really understand, had gotten away with a raccoon in a bag. Then they disappeared.

The python's tail was that same non-temperature, and although it tugged a little or wrapped itself around a support, it let Farrell pull it out, hand over hand. Then it wrapped itself around his arm, and Rose Marie said, "You unwrap it by the head. Here." Then she unwound the thing, put it back in the habitat, and slid the glass top over it.

Bob said, "Don't worry about my leg. I know a carpenter who can make a plug."

Back up in Laurel Canyon, they went through the privet hedge, like pistachio ice cream under a light, and stopped in front of Rose Marie's house. The car was quiet, but Farrell thought he could hear or sense the uneasy movement of the snake.

"So," she said. "You don't scare easily."

"I don't know," he said. "Let's take this thing upstairs."

They each took an end of the habitat, and with Farrell walking backward, they went in the door, up the stairs, and to the table where the tank usually sat. They put it down, and the snake raised its head.

"Well, at least it was exciting," Rose Marie said. "Gangsters, a rabid animal, a gunshot . . . is that the way it always is with you?"

"It's worse sometimes," he said.

A lot worse, he thought.

"There are things . . ."

"Like what?" she said.

"I don't know," he said. "This town hits you like I don't know what . . ."

In her bedroom, with the window open, with the sweet, human scent of their skin, still sweaty, in the slight breeze that came in the window, harsh with the aroma of manzanita, and yet scented with the roses, she turned to Farrell and said, "So, what is it you really do?"

Farrell put his hands behind his head. The ceiling was a blank white, the color of a piano key.

"You have to know?" he said.

"That's right, buster," she said.

"I don't want to lose you," he said. "That's what it comes down to."

She shrugged.

"It's up to you," she said. "I'm patient, but it isn't infinite."

15

FARRELL KNEW, WHEN HE GAVE Braumberg bad news, when he dropped the bomb on him, that the most important thing would be to stop Braumberg from doing something stupid. As far as Farrell was concerned, stupidity was applied panic, and that meant getting drunk and talking about things that should be kept quiet. The smart thing, Farrell knew, was to say nothing and be patient. The essence of panic was not knowing there were times when you should do nothing.

"We've got to stop meeting like this," said Farrell.

Braumberg turned to him with angry despair and said, "No jokes, huh?"

"Maybe we should meet at Pink's," said Farrell. "In the back."

"What? With all the grease hounds? I've got cholesterol problems. It's like getting a contact heart attack. No, right here is fine."

He touched the concrete bench at the fountain of the Hollywood Bowl.

All right, thought Farrell. Here it comes. Farrell had a fleeting recognition of the hangman at the trap. Was there a little thrill just before the drop? Is that what lingered now as he began to speak?

"There was another girl at Peregrine's," Farrell said. "A runaway."

"And?" said Braumberg.

"No one seems to know where she is," he said. "All I know is that she was from England."

"Maybe she caught the red-eye to England. Maybe she went home."

Farrell glanced from the greenish water in the fountain to Braumberg.

"Don't look at me that way," said Braumberg.

"She's not in England," Farrell said.

"So what now?"

"They're in a bad spot," Farrell said. "Peregrine and the girls."

"Tell me about that bad spot," Braumberg said.

"Well, they don't want to go to the cops, since this other girl is making them worry."

"Why do you suppose that is?" said Braumberg. "Oh, shit, stop looking at me that way."

"There are some possibilities," Farrell said.

"Great," said Braumberg. "You know, I think I should see a lawyer. What are we up to now? Conspiracy to obstruct justice? Accessories to some crime...?"

Braumberg's sweat, the color of baby oil, ran along the side of his face.

"You know what the problem with panic is," said Farrell. "It's doing something stupid."

"Is that right?" said Braumberg.

"Yes, it is," said Farrell.

"So, where is this girl from England?" said Braumberg.

Farrell thought of the dirt of the shoulder on Mulholland, the clutter of cigarette packages, foil, bindles, and the rest.

"I wish I knew," said Farrell.

"Well, she's a fucking runaway, the girl from England," said Braumberg. "Isn't that what you said? Isn't that what they do?"

"Yes, that's what they do," said Farrell.

"England. What a fucked-up place. You know what they eat there? Pickled walnuts. What can you expect?"

"I don't think we are talking about pickled walnuts," said Farrell.

"Maybe the whole thing will blow over. If they don't want to go to the cops, and Terry is making his morning calls, maybe we can just sit tight. You can give them some money . . ."

"You are beginning to sound like a teenaged girl," Farrell said. "It's the lines. You have to understand that. Get the lines."

"All right. All right," said Braumberg. "I'll cut Profonde a deal for an extra point, but that is going to make him suspicious."

"This is a town of suspicion," Farrell said. "And if you can't get the lines with Profonde, then get them for some other production in town. Right?"

Braumberg shrugged.

"Right?" said Farrell.

"All right, all right. Don't get shirty."

"Just get the lines," said Farrell.

"And what are you going to do?" said Braumberg.

"Look around for the girl," Farrell said.

"And if you find her?" said Braumberg.

"That's really the question," Farrell said. "Isn't it?"

"Shit," said Braumberg. "I've got a meeting. How do I look?"

"Great," Farrell said. "Calm, cool, collected. No one would try to pull a fast one on you. Those snakeskin boots are the best part."

"Have you got any Klonopin?" said Braumberg.

He took out the pillbox with Botticelli's Venus and opened it in the gurgling of the fountain so Braumberg could take a pill. Then the pillbox clicked shut, like finality itself.

Braumberg swallowed the pill dry. He sat on the edge of the fountain and stared at the line of cars that came up Highland, as though they would never end.

"Jesus, I don't know how Terry does it. You know what the makeup people are doing to make him look like he isn't all fucked out?"

"He's got great skin," Farrell said.

"Yeah, great skin," said Braumberg.

"You don't want to do something stupid," said Farrell. "In fact, you want to do something smart."

"What's that?" said Braumberg.

"Give more to institutions. The Children's Hospital at UCLA. It will do you a lot of good if this comes unglued."

"Don't say that," said Braumberg. "The unglued thing." He bit his lip, then glanced at Farrell. "You look tired."

"That's right," said Farrell. "The girls are lying. The mother is lying. Terry is lying. There's something wrong. I'm about ready to walk away . . ."

"Don't, don't," said Braumberg. "Don't even think about walking away. If you have to find out, all right."

"Then what?" Farrell said.

"Take care of it. Are you confused?"

"Not anymore," Farrell said.

"All right," Braumberg said. "Think about this. That hospital for kids seems important to you for some reason. Why is that?"

Farrell shrugged.

"Are you getting soft?"

"No," said Farrell.

"All right. You take care of this for me, and I will donate a substantial amount. Not for a building. But for research."

"How much?"

"A substantial amount. You want the fund in your name?"

"Are you kidding?" Farrell said. "No. How much?"

"Plenty. For tumor research. I got a fundraising pitch from them the other day and they are doing some good things with genetic sequencing, designer drugs for kids, you know, that work for each kid ..."

"It will do you good," said Farrell.

"On the condition that you take care of this. Think about it."

16

THE SUSPICION ABOUT WHY FARRELL hadn't been able to find the British girl came with a change in the way things appeared. In the afternoon he started with the habitual searching, the parking at the side of Mulholland, the repetitive climb into the brush, and his pushing at the toughness of the manzanita. The Australian perfume of the eucalyptus had appeared, in the usual method, as the evidence of frustration, but the instant he suspected what was wrong, the objects around him were oddly transformed. This change was similar to how a car morphed from something dependable to an item that couldn't be trusted when, say, a flat tire was discovered. Same car, but somehow different.

The certainty appeared out of that interior silence, that quiet darkness which exists before any idea that arrives without warning. Farrell felt it in his chest as a lightness, a buoyant awareness, like getting a joke, although he knew it was anything but a joke. The British girl wasn't there, or she hadn't been there, when he had looked. If she had been, he would have found her.

Farrell was working farther out on Mulholland, closer to the beach, when he looked up at that sky, as pale as a cataract, and realized a new possibility. He pushed through the brush, head down, something like a rugby player, back to the car, where, in the back seat he had the call sheet for Braumberg's picture, which had headings across the top that read "Time, Scene, Description, Cast, Location, Pages." Of course, the script wasn't shot in order, and Farrell flipped pages until he came the correct date. Terry's call was for a location in Downtown LA. An alley. Crew loads at 9:00 a.m.

Farrell backed into the shoulder, turned east, and drove until the houses were more visible, the pullouts less cluttered with evidence of what happened at night. A van was parked in front of Terry's house, and on the side was painted PERFECT POOL MAINTENANCE, REPAIR, ROBOT CLEANING. A cartoon of a swimming pool was below the words.

The pool attendant was a woman of about twenty-five who wore a pair of shorts, a khaki shirt, dark glasses, and was smoking a joint as she watched an automated vacuum cleaner work along the bottom of the pool. The machine seemed, in a way Farrell couldn't really explain, to enjoy the job, like a terrier going after a rat. The attendant had a pole and a sponge, which she was about to use on the sides of the pool where the robot couldn't reach.

Her nose ring was large, the tattoos on her arm were close to the color of the San Gabriel Mountains, dark to black, and the streak in her hair looked like the color of a pink lemonade Popsicle. At the back of the lower part of the house, a sliding door was unlocked, and at the entrance she had left a bottle of cyanuric acid and a plastic bucket, like the kind Sheetrock compound came in, that was filled with Trichlor tabs.

"Nice day," said Farrell.

"What's nice about it?" said the attendant.

"That cyanuric acid really helps," said Farrell.

"Just put it in," said the attendant.

"It protects the chlorine from ultraviolet rays," said Farrell.

"What are you, the Science Guy?" said the attendant.

"No," said Farrell. "Just a friend of Terry's."

"He has friends?" said the attendant. "Well, you should tell them to stop leaving condoms in the pool. It fucks up the robot. Guess who has to dig them out?"

"Not Terry," Farrell said. "That dope smells good."

"Here," she said. She held it out.

Farrell took a long drag, held it in his lungs, and then slowly exhaled.

"Where do you get this stuff?" said Farrell.

"Wouldn't you like to know?" she said.

"Whew," said Farrell.

She smiled.

"Without this stuff half the pools in this town wouldn't get cleaned."

"I left something here the other night," Farrell said.

"You want to go in?"

"Yes," said Farrell.

"Terry was all bent about me keeping my pool cleaning stuff in there," said the attendant. "About a week ago he was all antsy about it. But this morning, when I arrived, he said it was no big deal and I could store my stuff again. So, I guess it's all right. Go on in."

The room beyond the sliding door was dim, since the blinds were drawn. A large TV, a sofa, a table, a desk with a computer, an Eames chair and an ottoman, the laminated wood of them showing dark streaks. In the next room and through a sliding door, a small kitchen had been set up, along with a bar, and next to the bar was a flat freezer, about six feet long. Farrell stood in the doorway, that sense of knowing what he had missed as definite as a cool breeze. He opened the top. It was empty. The British girl hadn't been out there in the hills when Farrell had been looking. He guessed Terry had kept her in here for a while, and then pushed her into the brush. If that's what he did.

Farrell knew he'd have to start over. He had started too soon.

He took a hundred dollars out of his pocket and went back outside.

"Looks great," he said. He pointed at the pool.

"Did you find what you were looking for?" said the attendant.

In manner of speaking, thought Farrell.

"Here," he said. "You don't have to say anything either."

She put the money in the pocket of her khaki shirt, below the sewn-in script, in red thread, that read SASKIA.

"Thanks, Saskia," he said.

She frowned and said, "We're all Saskia. As long as we last."

"Take care," said Farrell.

"You better believe it," she said. "Just think about it. A million swimming pools waiting to be cleaned." She took a deep hit. "A million."

"Maybe you should look for another job."

She just stared at him, partly high, partly mesmerized by the robot in the pool.

"Now there's an idea."

Farrell got into his car and knew he'd have to start over. Terry had driven around with the British girl, then brought her back to his house to think about what to do, had driven up to the back door, and brought the British girl in where he could hide her for a while.

* * *

It didn't take long, now that Farrell had started searching again from the first locations. He expanded the radius of his search by another half mile. The body was not that far into the bushes, just enough to be invisible from the road. It was turned on its side and seemed as though it had not been dragged very far. She had on a white tank top with narrow straps for her shoulders, and over that she wore a short denim vest, cut with a wide opening at the bottom, like an upside-down V, and a wide opening at the top, like a V right side up. Only a short middle part of the vest, with three large brass buttons. The straps that held up the vest were dark cotton braids, which were almost childish, like something done as a project at a summer camp. Along with the tank top and the vest she wore dark jeans, not the bleached ones American kids wore, but an iris blue. Her running shoes had a sole with holes along the side, so that they appeared to have the texture of fish gills.

The girl had scratches on her shoulder where the skin wasn't covered by the tank top, but the scratches hadn't bled and were just dark lines. Farrell nodded as he thought, already wanting to look away, that this showed she had been dead when she had been left here. Of course, she lay at an unnatural angle, but why should it be any different? If a girl runs away from England, gets involved with people like the ones she so naturally found, as though gravity drew her to them, why should she look natural?

The sensation of being correct, or connected to the real world, came to Farrell as a change in his perception of light, and something else, too, which was a slight separation from the place where he stood, as though he had imagined it as much as discovered it. The British girl didn't look like she had been there for long, and the horrifying details of what happens after death were delayed by the cold of the freezer. It wouldn't be too much longer, though, for it to begin—odor, insects, swelling, those details that Farrell recoiled from, although he knew they were coming. Still, he had more time than he had previously thought he might.

But the problem was still there, as much as he wished otherwise.

A hawk floated over the Valley in the thermals above the smog. Its eyesight was so keen it could see a mouse even through the reddish air. Just like that, it occurred to Farrell that a hawk killed not by grabbing, but by hitting the thing it wanted so hard, with its talons, that they worked like a club.

Portia and Charlene had said the British girl had a tattoo. He put on a pair of latex gloves.

He didn't want to touch the brush, and he made sure none of his clothes was torn, not a shred of clothing left behind, at least from him. He didn't want to touch her, but then it could be a mistake, that is, this could be someone else altogether, since, after all, someone else could have killed another young woman in Los Angeles. She was just as light as he expected, and after she had been turned on her back, he unzipped the jeans and used a finger to pull her underwear down enough to see the tattoo. "Blessed is the man that heareth me . . ." Still clear, but the hair had grown a little, just like the beard of a man who will need a shave before he is buried.

He left her as she had been, clothes in order, although she still seemed to be lying in an awkward posture. Then he sat back on his haunches, and thought, So what am I left with now? Fury, is that it? Could he even say the word? The desire for vengeance? How had he come to this point, in the brush off Mulholland with this young woman? It all begins so easily, and yet, you can end up like this. *Bum*, he thought, is that what his father had meant? No, no, thought Farrell. He had never intended this. Never.

A small handbag, made of pale leather, but now appeared more like the color of a snake's belly, was in the brush near the girl's feet.

Farrell knew it was a felony, and a serious one, to tamper with evidence. But he picked up the bag, a round one like an enlarged compact, and turned the clasp. Aspinal was the brand name inside. He guessed this must have been a British brand, but there was no need to check it. Bland, ordinary cosmetics were inside, lipstick, shadow, a comb, an unopened packet of Kleenex, a couple of earrings that could have come from anyplace. He pushed them aside and at the bottom sat an Italian toothbrush, made of tortoiseshell, heavy, luxurious. The kind of brush a model in Rome might have. Next to it was a more ordinary, basic pharmacy toothbrush.

Farrell sat there for a moment, considering what this girl was trying to tell him, then went up to his car where he took a ziplock bag from the glove box, brought it back, and put the Italian toothbrush in it. The question was, had she used it? No, he thought, probably not.

A piece of dead brush was near the road, just a branch. Farrell started the car, drove it onto the hardtop, got out, and then used it to brush away the tracks of his shoes and the tread of the tires from the dirt of the shoulder. The branch went into the canyon.

He knew he shouldn't waste time, but he still stood opposite the Valley and the San Gabriel Mountains and strained to understand the meaning of "Blessed is the man that heareth me . . ." And what was that? What was she saying? What did she want Farrell to hear? Is this the last thing that could save him, this listening? Yes, he thought, that's what's working in the dark. The mood here, like transparent fog, was one he knew by its claustrophobia.

17

IN THE CAMRY, WITH ROSE Marie in the passenger seat, they went down to Sunset and turned right, toward the ocean. This part of town had gotten more run-down, just a memory of what it had been years ago. Junkies on the street, the usual desperation and false atmosphere, women in fishnet stockings, young men in tight-fitting jeans who were already hungry by early afternoon. Today, in the morning, they had the air of people waiting for a disaster they knew was coming.

"What's the rush?" said Rose Marie. "Why do you want to see the kids so soon?"

"I just thought I'd come along," he said.

"What's going on?"

"I wanted to see you and I wanted to come along," he said.

"Nothing else, huh?"

The door of the hospital, that enormous revolving cylinder, moved with its unstoppable motion, as though it was part of the inevitable. Farrell hadn't shaved, and the stubble on his face made a little static when he ran a hand over it. When they got out of the elevator Rose Marie said, "What are you trying to do? Look like a French actor? Sort of cute, though." She blinked. She leaned close, the scent of her hair strong, the touch of it soft and reassuring.

"I don't think I'm cute," he said.

"No, I guess not. Not with that scar in your eyebrow and that shopworn look. No, not cute."

The hall was clean and bright, the paint on the walls fresh.

"So, what's that tremble in your voice all about?"

"Th-th-is and that," he said.

The room was as before, a classroom, although the diagrams for math had been erased from the board. Now, "The Battle of Hastings" was written in large letters. "Offensive weapons triumphed over defense. Invaders had more archers than the defenders." The zing, the vibration of a bow string, seemed to linger as he stood there, considering a fight a thousand years ago while a dead girl was left in the brush at the side of the road.

Gerry, Catherine, Ann, and Jack were there, a sort of chorus, but somehow all the more powerful because they were young and seemed innocent. The definition of the difference between the way things appeared and the way they were.

"So, back again, huh? Just can't get enough of us, can you?" said Catherine.

"Most people who come here to see us are just faking it," said Ann. "They want to see us, but then they move on."

"I'm tired of things being faked," said Farrell.

"You know people like to do things for sick kids. Right?" said Gerry.

"Not really," said Catherine. "Once is usually enough. They pat themselves on the back, and that's it."

"What about that woman, the singer?" said Jack. "The blond . . . who came a couple of times?"

"Just as phony as the rest," said Catherine. "She just did a better job. And look at you. Slobbering over her. I thought the chemo killed hormones," said Catherine. "You better get down to the pharmacy and check your chemo. You're still all wired up on testosterone or something."

"Come on," said Rose Marie. She turned to Farrell. "Tell us a story."

"Yeah," said Gerry. "Something juicy. Some actor, you know, who is in deep trouble . . ."

"Let's talk about stuntmen," said Farrell.

"Isn't that what you do?" said Catherine. "Aren't you a sort of stuntman?"

"Let him talk," said Rose Marie, but her voice had an edge.

"In the old days, before digital effects and other tricks, stuntmen had to take some chances. For instance," Farrell said, "milk used to come in flat-topped cartons. The stuntmen would put out a mattress, cover it with a layer of the one-quart, flat-topped cartons, then put another mattress on top, then another layer of cartons, then another mattress. This was the best way to absorb energy when a stuntman had to take a fall from a second-story window. He hit the pile of mattresses, buffered by the collapsing layers of one-quart cartons. The stuntman would walk away."

"Wow," said Gerry. "Those days are gone."

"So, what's your milk carton?" said Catherine to Farrell.

Jack took off his hat and his scars were still pink, although a couple old ones were as white as fish bones.

"The stuntmen weren't afraid," said Jack.

Catherine turned to Farrell. "Do you get used to being afraid."

"Maybe," Farrell said.

Her dark eyes, her eyeliner, her white skin all the more uncanny than the last time. It was as though she was becoming more knowledgeable and more ethereal. She turned that glance on Farrell. It was like having the light of a prison swing over someone who is trying to escape.

"You've come back so soon," she said.

"Yes," he said.

"Those stuntmen were a dying breed," she said.

They were quiet for a moment, not glancing at each other or the walls or the windows, either. Catherine sat there, her dark eyes with that odd, almost beam-like presence.

"You don't lie," she said to Farrell. "That's important to us. What's the percentage in lying to us? There's none." She kept on looking at Farrell. "So, what are you really doing?"

"Work," he said.

"What kind of work do you really do?" said Catherine. "If you don't talk . . ." She gestured to Rose Marie. "We will tell her not to bring you around anymore."

"No lies," said Ann.

"I try to get people out of trouble," he said.

"You mean like actors and stuff," said Catherine. "You always read about them taking drugs, rehab, quack, quack, quack."

"I've worked with other people, too. Like baseball players. Athletes."

"I bet they really fuck up," said Jack.

"Language," said Rose Marie.

"Well, you know what?" said Jack. "If this guy hasn't heard the word, it's about time he did. And if he has, one more time isn't going to hurt him."

Catherine giggled.

"You know there aren't many people like you," Farrell said to them.

"How's that?" said Catherine.

"I can trust you," Farrell said.

"You better believe it," said Jack.

"So, what's the problem?" said Catherine.

"It's hard to say," Farrell said.

"Oh, screw that," said Jack. "If you can't make it real, then it's not a problem, right?"

"Right," said Catherine.

"Well, yes and no," Farrell said.

"Don't get slippery," said Catherine.

"Yeah," said Jack.

"Make it concrete or go home," said Catherine. She began to cry a little, not much, and then touched the side of her face with the back of her hand.

Don't fail them, he thought. What would it feel like to walk out of here and not be able to come back?

"Let's say you get into something for a simple reason. You think a lot of people are in trouble because they are judged by hypocrites. You know, you use a drug, you sleep with someone's wife, or husband, you make a promise you don't keep, you get married more than once without getting a divorce, you hide the fact that you have a kid, that you stole some money, that you have been in jail, and the people who judge you do the same thing. And they want to ruin you for it."

"Sure," said Catherine. "Sure. But that's just the beginning."

She knows, thought Farrell.

"After a while it gets complicated," said Catherine. "It was pretty clear, then it got gray, then ..."

"Dark," said Farrell.

"And you're in the darkness now ..." said Catherine.

He shrugged.

"Yes," he said.

"So, get out," she said.

In their glance Farrell saw that glassine clarity between them.

"Uh-oh," she said. "I get it. You've become part of it. Is that it?"

"I wish I knew," he said. "If you say you are going to do something, and then you don't do it, are you still the same person as when you said you would?"

"No," said Catherine. "You're a punk. Especially if it's a promise like the one you made to me."

"It's not that kind of promise," said Farrell.

"So?" said Catherine.

"What if the thing you said you were going to do has changed, or what you have to do to finish the job has changed? And that even though things have changed, other people might benefit if you keep the commitment."

"You mean like a lot more serious?" said Catherine.

"Yeah," he said.

"You are just trying not to be less of a person," she said. "Is that it?"

Rose Marie kept her eyes on Farrell.

"Listen to this," said Catherine. "We had some jackass in here the other day from UCLA philosophy. Like he wanted to talk philosophy with us. He talked about Hegel."

"I've read a little," Farrell said. "A little heavy going sometimes."

"You might read what he has to say about tragic heroes," Catherine said.

"What's that?" he said.

"Look it up," she said.

"I haven't got the time," said Farrell.

"I don't want to show off," she said. "But then, you know, you're scared shitless. That's something I know about."

"That's right," Farrell said. "I'm trying not to show it though."

"It's like this," said Catherine. "You want the heart of it? What the jackass from UCLA gave us? See, a man can have a lot of obligations. To his family, to his wife, to society, to himself. And mostly they work together."

"Do you remember what that was called . . ." said Rose Marie.

"Apa . . . something," said Jack.

"Apollonian," said Rose Marie.

"Yeah, that's it. When it all works together. But every now and then something goes wrong. The obligations are opposed to one another. Does that sound familiar?"

"Yeah," Farrell said.

"The tragic hero, according to the UCLA jackass, will stick with only one. The other bonds pulled him down."

"Okay," Farrell said.

"All that shit is gone," said Jack. "It's like the stuntmen. Bunch of dead ducks."

They had that stare again, not at the walls, not at the window, not at each other.

Catherine put her hand, so cool and white, on Farrell's arm. Just for a moment, as though she wanted to take a temperature, or to feel the warmth of someone who was healthy.

"I understand," she said. "Just by touching you. I don't want to go downstairs tomorrow and let them put some more of that poison into me. That chemotherapy. It's cold when it goes in."

"Yes," Farrell said. "I believe you."

"But I have to do it, to go on being me," she said. "Because if I don't, then I . . ."

She shrugged.

"I won't be here anymore to give you shit," she said.

The others laughed. But not Rose Marie.

"And you like that?" Farrell said. "Giving me shit?"

"I love it," said Catherine.

"Well," he said. "That's a relief."

She smiled. But her eyes had that same dark light sweep, like the negative of a lighthouse.

"So, tell me," said Catherine. "Details."

"I can't do that," Farrell said.

"I guess that means someone died," said Catherine. "But I won't push you."

"Maybe it was a mistake," Farrell said.

"Don't you hope," said Catherine. "You're looking at a walking, talking mistake." She shrugged in the direction of the others. "Them, too."

Rose Marie said, "Let's talk about something else."

Catherine went on staring at Farrell.

"You can run away," she said. "But that's not going to help, not long term. You're like one of us. You've got something and you can't fix it. Welcome to the club."

The sensation of this particular trap was at once soft as a cloud and yet like being caught in barbed wire, since Farrell's constantly changing estimation of it left him aware that in addition to the facts, he was trapped by his mood.

"Rose Marie wouldn't think much of you if you ran away," Catherine said.

"You know what I'd like to be," said Gerry. "I'd like to be a homicide detective."

He looked right at Farrell.

"Good luck," said Catherine.

"We've got to go watch a movie downstairs," said Jack. "A romantic comedy. Girl gets boy. Girl loses boy. Girl gets boy. Just like clockwork."

"Everything goes like clockwork here. Everything is figured in terms of time."

"Survival rates," said Jack. "How many years, months, weeks?"

Then the kids got up and went to the door, although Catherine looked back at Farrell. "It's simple, really. Just do the right thing."

In the hall their footsteps were like those of a small herd of goats.

In the elevator, when they were alone, Rose Marie said, "You can cry if you want. It's only me."

"I'll save it for later."

From the parking lot the aluminum and glass of the building were dull in the California light.

"I thought you were going to save that for later," she said.

"Some things can't wait," he said. "They're good kids."

"Yes," she said. "They are. And they like you, too."

18

FARRELL KNEW THAT THE MOST dangerous creature is a weak man who is terrified. And, as though he needed proof, as he sat at the long table in Philippe's, he guessed that Terry would try to kill him soon. In the smell of Philippe's French dip sandwiches, in the sawmill-like atmosphere of the sawdust on the floor and the white, ceramic pots of mustard on the tables, Farrell was more certain than ever that Terry would try to kill him soon. The restaurant had a counter where people ordered sandwiches, on French bread with roast beef or pork, and the patrons got a glass of water that was filled by pushing a tumbler against a black bumper beneath a spigot. Behind the counter tubs of potato salad had stripes of paprika on the top, orangish lines that were at once festive and comforting. The mustard in the pots was so hot it made Farrell's eyes water, but he hadn't had any today. He'd only had a cup of coffee, in a heavy ceramic cup, just like the pots for mustard. He waited, eyes on the door.

Terry came in, his dark glasses round and stylish, his Armani T-shirt and his black jeans making him seem like someone who was posing as an actor not wanting to be seen. He stood next to Farrell and said, "So, what's the big deal?"

"I just wanted you to buy me a sandwich," said Farrell. "Will you buy me lunch?"

"I'll buy you lunch," said Terry. "What's it going to be?"

"A French dip sandwich," said Farrell.

Terry stood at the counter, where the women in brown uniforms with white aprons made sandwiches, their manner something like that of a nurse. As Terry waited, he picked at his fingernails, shifted his weight, looked around, and then tapped a toe, not with impatience but uneasiness. After he paid, Terry came back to the table and shoved the sandwich at Farrell. Terry had one for himself, too.

Terry pulled up a stool, which made four lines, one from each leg, in the sawdust on the floor. Farrell put mustard on the sandwich with the tongue depressors that were in the pots of mustard. His eyes watered.

"Hot, isn't it?" said Terry.

"Yes," said Farrell.

"So, what's the big deal?"

His eyes lingered over Farrell's face, as though looking for a hint, a clue that the time had come.

"So, Braumberg has got the lines," Farrell said. "Profonde's AD will call the girls and give them their lines. They're going to have to show up tomorrow to get a costume and to see where they are going to work."

"Profonde's assistant director knows more about movies than he does. She is really doing the work, you know that?" said Terry.

"Yes," said Farrell. "If you say so. But they've got their parts."

"So, that's it, right?" said Terry. "We're making progress, right?"

Farrell took the postcard from his pocket and put it on the table next to the pot of hot mustard.

"Yeah," said Terry. "I'm glad to see that. I was going to ask for it back."

"I'd like to ask you about it," said Farrell.

"What's to say?" said Terry.

"Do you notice anything funny about it?"

"No," said Terry. "A card from a dippy girl from Alaska."

"Uh-huh," said Farrell. "She hasn't contacted you has she? No calls, no more cards, no letter from Alaska?"

"No," said Terry. He sat perfectly still, his fingers holding his sandwich but not moving. Alert, looking around, then back at Farrell. "She's not trying to put the bite on me, too, is she?"

"I don't know," said Farrell.

"Do you think she might?" said Terry.

Farrell thumbed the edge of the card, flipped it over so the hearts and smiley faces for the *i*'s were visible. Then back to the picture of the bear.

"No," said Farrell. "After thinking about it, no, I don't."

"What's to think about?" said Terry. "She got tired of LA, went back to fish land, the Land of the Midnight Sun, and that's it. Hasta la vista."

Farrell put the card back in his pocket.

"I think I'd like to have that," said Terry.

"I'll keep it for a while," said Farrell.

"It was sent to me," said Terry.

"I'll keep it," said Farrell. "For safety's sake."

"For safety's sake?" said Terry. "No. I want it."

"What's the big deal?" said Farrell. "It's just a card from a girl who went home to Alaska."

"Let me decide about that," Terry said.

"It's supposed to be proof that she got home, right?"

"Yeah," said Terry. He swallowed, looked around, picked at his face, then at his fingers. "Give."

"Let's talk about the British girl," said Farrell.

"I told you about that," said Terry. "That's gone and done with. Ancient history. Why are you harping on that?"

"You haven't heard anything from her? No telephone calls?" said Farrell.

"No," said Terry. "Why would she call me?"

Farrell nodded. "No postcards?"

Farrell didn't wait for an answer.

"No. I wouldn't think so. How could she?" he said.

"Give me the card," said Terry.

"You know, in California, they still have the gas chamber," said Farrell.

"For the people dumb enough to get caught," said Terry. "But they are talking about a moratorium."

"That's a lucky break," said Farrell. "For those stupid enough to get caught."

"Listen," said Terry. "I didn't have anything to do with that British twit. Nothing. If she got into trouble it wasn't me. I'm telling you the truth. No ifs, ands, or buts. That's the way it is."

"You're sure?" said Farrell.

"I don't like your tone," said Terry. "First you were supposed to help me with a small problem and now you are pushing me around. Just who are you working for?"

Farrell shrugged.

"Me? I'm working for me," Farrell said.

"Well, you better snap out of it," said Terry.

"Here's the message," said Farrell. "You make your early calls, finish the picture, keep your nose clean, and then I'll finish with the trouble. The girls will get their lines. They aren't going to do anything . . . not for a while."

"I want the card," said Terry.

"Just make your morning calls," said Farrell. "Then we'll talk."

Terry rocked back and forth his stool, pushed his sandwich, on a paper plate, one way and then another. He looked in a mustard pot as though something important was there and turned a look of rage on Farrell. But he didn't do anything about it. He smiled, nodded, and said, "People always underestimate me. How could a fluffer ever get where I am, right?"

"Right," said Farrell.

"I don't give warnings," said Terry.

"I know," said Farrell.

"And you are going to keep that card?"

"That's right," said Farrell. "Just make your calls and finish your job."

"And all that talk about the gas chamber is just to scare me. Well, I don't scare easily."

"I know," said Farrell. "They're talking about a moratorium."

Terry looked at his hands.

"No one is going to take anything away from me."

"Sure," said Farrell. "Just make your calls in the morning."

"I'll do that," said Terry.

"Thanks for the lunch."

"I hope you enjoyed it," said Terry. "I really do."

"Just make your calls. There aren't that many shooting days left."

"Yeah," said Terry. "Not many days left to do the shooting."

He stood and pulled his dark glasses down, which had been on his head like a knight's visor, and then stood next to the table, the dark lens with a dot of light in them. He put his finger under the paper plate for Farrell's sandwich, and began to tip it into Farrell's lap.

"I wouldn't to that if I were you," said Farrell.

"Maybe some other time," said Terry, who turned and went out the door, his shoes leaving prints in the sawdust as though it was a thin layer of new snow. Farrell took the two plates to the trash, threw them in, and then stood at the counter, where a woman in one of those brown dresses with a white apron stood, a fork in her hand as she was about to stab one of the roasts she carved for the sandwiches.

"Can you do me a favor?" said Farrell. "My friend and I were having a business lunch. He forgot his receipt for his credit card. Can you give me a copy?"

The woman had brown hair with streaks of gray, lines around her eyes and in the middle of her forehead from years of frowning at the people who came into Philippe's.

"What are you, an accountant?"

"Yes," said Farrell. "That's right."

"That guy with the dark glasses who was trying to look like an actor who doesn't want to be recognized."

"That's the one," said Farrell.

"We keep a duplicate," said the woman. She reached into the cash register and pulled one out.

"Here," she said.

She passed it over and felt the folded hundred-dollar bill that Farrell had in his hand.

"Well," she said. "Isn't that sweet? I didn't think accountants were so generous."

"The world is filled with surprises," he said.

The traffic was as always, nonstop cars and buses, all jammed into a place that was too small, and so it took Farrell about a half hour to get to Cahuenga Boulevard and to the office of Charles Dent. Downstairs in the square plaza, with its Miracle-Gro palms and those hibiscus flowers that were so bright as to look like blooms in an animated cartoon, the sunlight fell with a mustard color.

Farrell knocked on the door, and when Dent opened, Farrell said, "Don't you ask first who's at the door."

"I saw you on the surveillance camera," said Dent. "So, you need something, right?"

Farrell gave him the credit card receipt. The last four numbers were visible, and the bank it was drawn on.

"And?" said Dent.

"I'd like the charges on it for the last month," said Farrell.

"Sit down," said Dent.

Farrell sat on the sofa opposite the desk, which seemed like one you would find in the VIP lounge of an airport. Not really comfortable, not really new, but keenly anonymous. Dent typed and looked at his monitor.

"What's happening over there?" said Farrell. He gestured to the wall.

"The shrink? Same old, same old, divorce, an emergency room visit with a strange object in a rectum, addiction, anxiety, worry about not being good enough looking, saying the wrong thing. The usual."

"What was in the rectum," said Farrell.

"A cue ball," said Dent. "Won't be long before I have the password. Hang on a minute."

"Okay," said Farrell. "A couple of minutes?"

"Yeah," said Dent. "And they call this security. Jesus."

Uh-huh.

Dent gestured to the wall behind him, the shrink's office.

"You know what the basic problem is?" said Dent.

"No," said Farrell. "What is it?"

"People think they know what they want, but they don't."

"Maybe it's not enough," said Farrell.

"Sure," said Dent. He was so anonymous it was difficult to look at him and think he was still there, as though he was going to vanish somehow into the paint behind him. "It's like the baseball player, a pitcher, who was best friends with an outfielder."

"So?" said Farrell.

"So, the outfielder dies and the pitcher is heartbroken. But one day, the pitcher is standing on the mound and he hears the voice of the outfielder. The pitcher says, 'Wow, wow, great to hear from you. What's heaven like?' The outfielder says, 'Just great. We play a doubleheader every day and the ball never takes a bad bounce.' 'That's wonderful,' says the pitcher. 'Yeah,' says the outfielder. 'There's only one problem. You're pitching tomorrow night.'"

Muted voices came from the office next door. Not quite an argument but some vibrant intensity.

"Bingo," said Dent. "There it is. What do you want to know? He just had lunch at Philippe's. Great French dip sandwiches."

"What about travel?" said Farrell.

"A few weeks ago he bought a ticket to Alaska."

"Alaska," said Farrell.

"Yeah, you know, bears and salmon and dark winters. You don't look happy. You need something more?"

"The name on the ticket," said Farrell.

"You don't think I can get that?" said Dent.

"I didn't say it," said Farrell.

"The airlines think they are so cool," said Dent. "But they aren't. You want the name on the boarding pass."

Farrell nodded, yes, yes.

Dent worked at the keyboard. Waited.

"A guy by the name of Karicek."

"Round trip?" said Farrell.

"That's right," said Dent. "Came back on the same day."

Farrell sat in his car with the credit card record and the copy of a boarding pass. The date was the same as the postmarked card with the picture of the bear on it.

19

THE BROOKLYN BRIDGE MOTEL WAS on the Pacific Coast Highway in Manhattan Beach. Its rooms were fanned around a pool in what Farrell thought of as a California courtyard. Farrell parked by the pool.

A bundle of five thousand dollars was in the false bottom of the glove box, and when Farrell took them out, they were too thick for his wallet. So, as at other times, he put the bundle into a cheap envelope. Farrell put the envelope into the large pocket of the fishing shirt he wore. He wasn't a fisherman but the big pockets were handy. The morning was misty, but by afternoon the light would look like it was being filtered through cigarette smoke in a bar at 4:00 a.m.

In the trunk of the Camry, Farrell moved some tools around, a box in which he had some screwdrivers, a set of sockets, an adjustable wrench, a cordless drill, and a bolt cutter with jaws like a snapping turtle. Or anything that could really bite.

Karicek's room was on the second floor, in the middle of the building, which meant that he could run two ways along the veranda in front of the doors of the rooms. The railing, like the pipes used for handrails in prisons, went around the veranda. It had rusted in the salty air, and the blistering of it suggested the unstoppable impact of this place.

The venetian blinds made a little click behind the window as Karicek moved them to see who had knocked.

"What do you want?" Karicek said through the door.

"I've got some money for you."

Farrell waited at the door. He knew Karicek had every reason to wonder about strangers offering things to him. Still, it was possible that people from something like Publishers Clearing House were offering deals on magazines. Farrell thought Karicek was probably a sucker for a deal on magazines.

"This isn't a good time," said Karicek.

"You'd be surprised," Farrell said.

More silence behind the door.

"Yeah?" said Karicek. "Why would I be surprised?"

"I'd like to talk to you about that."

"I've got to be careful these days," said Karicek.

Farrell put the envelope of money against the window, where Karicek had spread the venetian blinds. The parallel lines of the slats looked like the spreading fronds of a palm in a jungle.

Farrell flipped the used, dirty bills like a deck of cards, gestured at the handles of the bolt cutter that stuck out of the gym bag that Farrell had put on the veranda. Karicek's eyes glanced down at the red handles with the black grips.

Karicek produced a Buck knife, which he opened and locked. He used the blade to hold the blinds open. Then he opened the door a little. Farrell came closer. Just a couple of inches were between them.

"What's that?" Karicek said. He pointed at the red handles of the bolt cutter.

"You're wearing a tracking bracelet, aren't you?"

Karicek opened the door. Farrell came into the room.

The scent of cigarette smoke came out of the air conditioner, and the sanitation bar in the toilet gave the room a sickly air.

"I've talked to the cops already," he said.

"I'm not a cop," Farrell said.

"No," Karicek said. "A cop wouldn't have a bolt cutter. And he wouldn't have money."

The bag sat on the floor.

"My name's . . ." Farrell said.

"Let me guess," said Karicek. "Mr. Jones, right? No one uses a real name with me. Sure. Sure. Nice to meet you Mr. Jones. Close the door. Like I say, I've got to be careful these days. They think I have something to do with five-year-olds. I don't get involved with anyone that young. That's the truth."

"Sure."

"They've got to be women," he said. "You know?"

"I know," Farrell said.

It seemed to Farrell that the air was getting heavier. He considered Nemesis, or other gods who dispensed justice. How vain the gods must have been when they brought vengeance.

The sofa, the chair, the paint-by-number landscapes on the wall, the empty bags of fast food, of Chinese takeout, which Karicek had eaten with a plastic fork stuck in some chow mein, the drab carpet were perfectly generic. Karicek put the knife, locked open, on the table next to the white boxes of the Chinese takeout.

"You don't look happy," said Karicek.

Karicek had pulled the blinds shut and the room was lighted by a sixty-watt bulb in a lamp. A fluorescent glow came from the bathroom. Karicek was in his late twenties, with long hair, which he wore in a ponytail. A gold earring. A tattoo of a snake, a boa, wrapped around his neck. On his ankle he had a GPS bracelet. It looked like a robot's love charm.

"No," Farrell said. "I'm not happy."

"That makes two of us," said Karicek. "I'm not happy. I don't want much, not really."

Farrell took the money out of the envelope and put it on the table next to a box of pork lo mein.

"This is a new one," said Karicek, as he touched the bracelet on his ankle. "For a while the old one didn't work. No signal. So, they came this morning and changed them."

He looked at the money with an expression at once needy and terrified.

Farrell picked up the money.

"Hey, hey," said Karicek.

Someone walked by the door on the veranda outside, and Karicek stiffened, turned his ear toward the door.

"You know," Farrell said. "You've got some trouble."

Karicek stroked his ponytail, as though that would bring him luck. Everything about him, even if tawdry, had the air of a fetish.

"You've been convicted before on child endangerment and sex with minors. A number of times."

"Well, what can I say?" said Karicek.

"Tell me," said Farrell. "When you are locked up, what do you do? You have to be pretty alone."

"Yeah," said Karicek. "I don't mind. It's safer."

"But what do you do?"

"I've got a hobby," said Karicek.

"A hobby?" said Farrell.

"Yeah?" said Karicek. "I think about cars. Building them. Buying parts for them. And you know something? All the parts catalogues come to prison. No trouble. Not like lingerie companies."

"Car parts?" said Farrell. "Well you are going to have plenty of time to think about them. Sex with minors and child endangerment."

"All bullshit," said Karicek. "Jesus, the girl looked eighteen."

"I'd say they looked fourteen," Farrell said.

"You've been talking to the cops, right?"

"No. Let's just say I've had some experience."

"Jesus," said Karicek. "Everyone in this town does it."

"Like your brother?" said Farrell.

"My what?"

"Your brother," said Farrell. "Let's talk about him."

"How do you know about that?" said Karicek.

"And let's talk about the British girl," said Farrell.

Karicek sat back, put his hand on his ponytail, considered Farrell with an expression that was so familiar, so much like Terry's, as to be uncanny. His fingers touched the knife, as though thinking it over.

"What about her?" said Farrell.

Karicek shook his head, but it was hard to tell if it meant, No, I don't know anything about this, or No, I don't believe anyone knows.

"I love my brother," said Karicek. "You know that?"

"And when did you start seeing underage girls?" said Farrell. "In West Virginia? The two of you."

"What are you after?"

"Let's just talk it over," said Farrell.

"Yeah," said Karicek. "West Virginia. But you've got to realize you are taking a chance. A big one."

"You're already in so much trouble there's not much you can do."

"If I am, what's a little more trouble?"

"So, you were there the other night?"

"Define 'there'?" said Karicek.

"Terry's house. With the British girl."

"You're taking a chance," said Karicek.

"But Terry didn't take her to the doctor. You did. Right?"

Karicek moved from side to side, poked at one of the cold Chinese takeout boxes.

"No," said Karicek. "I didn't. He wanted me to, but I didn't. I love him, but I already helped him before. No. That British twit was his problem. He took care of it, not me."

"Was she alive when you left her at Terry's?" said Farrell.

"She was fucked up," said Karicek. "I didn't want anything to do with it."

"But you helped him before?"

Karicek looked at the stale pork lo mien.

"You know why I love my brother? Do you know what it takes to get from a shithole like we grew up in . . . to a place like Terry's in?"

"I think I do," said Farrell.

"No, you don't," said Karicek. "You think you do but you don't."

"And when Terry was out here and you followed him, you found the young girls for him, didn't you?"

"So what?"

He touched the knife.

"Terry couldn't start hanging around in the juice bars on Sunset. He'd be recognized," said Farrell. "And what were you doing in Alaska?"

"Taking care of a problem," said Karicek.

"Like this?"

Farrell held out the postcard.

"Yeah," said Karicek.

"This card ties you, Terry, and the Alaskan girl together . . . you see that?"

"I love Terry," said Karicek. "Even though he's ashamed of me. He uses me, but I don't mind. I love him. There's only one problem. He doesn't give me much money. It's like he still holds it against me that I got a used bike for Christmas when he didn't get anything."

"You know, people are looking for the girl from Alaska," said Farrell.

"Have they found her?" said Karicek.

"So you know she's somewhere to be found," said Farrell.

"Oh, boy," said Karicek. "You are a piece of work. You really are on the ragged edge of thinness."

Karicek kept his eyes on the money, which was the color of tattoo ink.

"You're facing the three strikes and you're out problem," said Farrell. "Murder one. Not to mention that as a sex offender, they're going to keep you . . . for a long time."

"So you're a fucking lawyer," said Karicek.

"No. I'm just telling you the way that's going to work out. This isn't like gambling or stealing credit card numbers or making phony IDs. This isn't like that. Period. This isn't could-be life. This will be life in a place like Pelican Bay."

Karicek put his finger on the money.

"They're talking about a moratorium on the death penalty."

"Good news, huh?" said Farrell.

"And you're supposed to be helping Terry? Is that it?"

"I'm looking into it," said Farrell.

"Hang on a minute," said Karicek.

He tapped a number in his phone, poked at the stale lo mein while a number rang, then looked directly at Farrell.

"Yeah, Terry, it's me. I know, I know. I wouldn't call if I didn't need to. I know you're busy. Yeah. I've got a Mr. Jones here? I don't know how he found out, but he knows. Maybe he found out by knowing someone in West Virginia."

He was silent for a moment.

"Okay," said Karicek. "I'll do that."

Karicek hung up, then looked at Farrell and then down at the money.

"He's not happy," said Karicek. "Not happy at all."

"He's going to be worse if you don't make sure about the girl from Alaska."

"Like how?" said Karicek. "Just sort of as a thought exercise. How?"

"It's important for Terry that she's not found," said Farrell.

Karicek blinked as he concentrated.

"That she's properly hidden," said Farrell. "And that she doesn't have her identification on her. A wallet. Did you take that?"

"I don't know what you are talking about," said Karicek.

"The wallet should not be there," said Farrell.

"And how would someone wearing this take care of anything?"

He put out his leg to show the ankle monitor. Farrell took the bolt cutter from the bag and put it on the table.

"That's manageable," Farrell said.

Outside, on the highway, a motorcycle went by, the whine of it almost impossibly high, like an instrument from a tribe in the Himalayas. If the window had been open the scent of the ocean, mixed with the exhaust of the Pacific Coast Highway would come in.

"You know what they do to child molesters in a place like San Quentin? Or Pelican Bay?"

"I'd go for protective custody," said Karicek.

"Well, there will come a day when you have to share a shower or an exercise pod, or go to the doctor, the infirmary, something like that, and . . ."

"So?"

"You know how to make a spike out of a toothbrush? It's as good as an ice pick. But I think in your case it's more likely a matter of being slashed. A razor blade in a melted comb or toothbrush or something like that. Here."

Farrell pointed to the money-colored tattoo on Karicek's neck. That boa.

"You think when someone got guillotined and the head was in the basket it had time to know what was happening?" Farrell said.

Another motorcycle went by.

"So you cut this thing off," said Karicek. He ran his finger over the ankle monitor. "What do I give you?"

"You make sure about the girl from Alaska. That way, Terry isn't going to get dragged into anything."

"Are you talking about honor," said Karicek. "Me taking care of my brother?"

Honor?

"Your hands are shaking," said Karicek.

"Are th-th-they?"

"Yeah," said Karicek.

"You say you love your brother?"

Karicek nodded.

"Good. I give you a little walking around money. Cut off the bracelet. You do the honorable thing. Maybe you'll escape what's waiting at Pelican Bay."

Karicek put his head down, held his ponytail, then rubbed his neck.

"You never think you are going to end up like this," said Karicek.

"I understand," said Farrell.

On the shelf behind him were three books. *Young Love, Forever a Teen,* and *Picking Winners at the Track . . ."*

"What about those girls in the house?" said Karicek. "And that British item?"

"They've been taken care of," said Farrell.

"And Terry won't get hurt?" said Karicek.

The bracelet came off with a little click, like the sound of fate, which always reveals itself in the smallest detail. At least in the beginning, in the first appearance.

"Well," Farrell said. "Good luck."

"Sure," said Karicek. "Same to you."

Karicek held out his hand. They stood opposite each other, and Farrell thought of the gladiators, who said, "morituri te salutamus . . ." We who are about to die salute you. He took Karicek's hand and shook it.

"If they find the girl from Alaska, or if she isn't hidden properly," said Farrell. "It will come back to Terry, and when that happens, it will come back to you."

Karicek sat down and put his head in his hands, and when he looked up, his eyes showed the true depths of awareness of what he was facing.

It must have been like looking through a telescope at the images of the depths of space. All mystery, all chill, even beautiful in a way, that is, if you thought reality could be beautiful.

The door wasn't locked, and it opened with a hush as the bottom of it ran over the shag carpet of the room. Karicek looked up as Farrell did, and Nikolay, with his formfitting T-shirt and those arms that looked like water balloons under the skin, and Pavel, with that acne like a gray surface of the moon, came into the room. They stood for a moment, sniffing the air, glancing at those white boxes, with corners like an envelope, that were filled with stale Chinese food. Nikolay moved his eyes, as though they were something like a metal detector, to the money on the table.

"Hey, Farrell," said Pavel.

Farrell nodded. Karicek still held his head in his hands but he was now sweating, the icy sheen of moisture visible on his skin.

"You know," said Nikolay. "Our friend doesn't look so good, does he?"

"And this other one," said Pavel, his acne covered face showing disdain, looking at Karicek, "doesn't look so good either."

"So, you followed me?" said Farrell.

"Why you must be getting dotty. Of course, we did," said Nikolay. "You don't think we believed that you were in the vending machine business because you liked Doritos."

"Someone is in the vending machine business for one thing. They are hiding something," said Pavel.

They both turned to Karicek.

"So, who's this unhappy fuck?" said Nikolay. "Looks pretty scared. What's he done?"

"It's got to be something," said Pavel. "Show me the man and I will show you the fear."

"That's not quite right," Nikolay said. "It was Stalin's man, Beria, who said, 'Show me the man and I will show you the crime.'"

"Beria was dead way before we were born. Strictly old school. But he had a point," said Pavel.

Farrell wondered if they knew that Beria was hung not only for crimes in the cheka but because he had been a rapist who had his underlings grab women off the streets of Moscow. Now, this suspicion added to Farrell's alertness, or his awareness that these two were more sinister than he had given them credit for. Maybe he was losing his touch.

Nikolay looked at the money on the table again, and then picked up a box of Chinese takeout.

"Noodles. Can't hold a candle to pelmeni."

He pushed it aside and turned to Farrell.

"So what are you doing?"

"I get people out of trouble."

"Well, that sounds like a growth industry. Glad to hear it. What's this guy done?"

"I just want to be left alone," said Karicek.

"We're here to help you with that," said Pavel.

"He has a warrant out for his arrest," said Farrell.

"For what?"

"He's been dealing in stolen car parts. He has a collection of dealers who buy from him. A network."

"And so his boss is paying you to get him away, so he won't rat anyone out? Is that it?"

Farrell nodded. It was comforting, at least, to deal with people who thought in a definite way, betrayal, shaking someone down, bullying. At least you knew what they would believe. Most of the time.

"Auto parts?" said Pavel. He touched those scars on his face. "Seems like there should be something more than that in this town. All those characters with kinky habits. Gerbils. Underage girls."

"I guess you hear rumors," said Farrell.

"Yeah," said Nikolay. "Who knows what these people are up to? Something's off."

"Yeah," said Karicek. "But this is just car parts."

Pavel and Nikolay each crossed his arms across his chest, the gesture so similar as to look like Russian nesting dolls. They went on staring at Karicek.

"So, tell me, what does a new Corvette fuel pump go for?"

Karicek sat now with his hands in his lap.

"You mean a Delphi gasoline pump?" said Karicek.

"Yeah. If that's what it is. A Delphi," said Nikolay.

"From an auto parts store," said Karicek. "About three-fifty. That's ballpark."

"Look it up," said Nikolay.

Pavel took his phone from his pocket, typed in the name of the pump and said, "Fuck. My thumbs are so big." Then he got it right. They waited. Karicek glanced at Farrell.

"Bingo," said Pavel. "Three-fifty."

They all were silent, considering the price of the pump. Then Nikolay sighed and said, "All right."

"So, you thought you were pretty smart, didn't you?" said Pavel.

"Not if you're here," said Farrell.

"We'll call it even," said Pavel.

"For our cut," said Nikolay. "And this guy can go sell his fuel pumps."

Farrell picked up the money from the table, counted out a thousand dollars. Nikolay took it, flipped the bills back and forth, smelled them, and said, "Nothing like that scent. Nothing. You want to smell?"

He held it out for Farrell.

"I know what it smells like," said Farrell.

"I bet you do," said Pavel.

"Hasta la vista," said Nikolay. "In LA-speak. See you around, smart guy."

They went out the door, their gait identical, half swagger, half stalking, like a mixture of a gorilla and a cobra. They pulled the door shut with that same rough brushing sound.

Karicek and Farrell waited for a moment.

"Friends of yours?" said Karicek.

"I wouldn't go that far," said Farrell.

"Okay," said Karicek. "I'll see what I can do."

Farrell walked to the door, opened it, and went into that gray luminescence. The pool was empty, and the outside walkway was deserted. The only movement was a jet trail, a sort of white mark in the sky, like a scratch on the fender of a blue car. The flower box in front of the motel was filled with black dirt, where geraniums grew, and Farrell wiped off the ankle bracelet and pushed it into the flower box.

* * *

The Mist House was on Santa Monica Boulevard, about twenty minutes from the Brooklyn Bridge motel. It was an old-style restaurant with booths, linen table cloths, waiters in white shirts and aprons. It was cool in the afternoon, before the rush, and the barman was slicing lemons, cleaning glasses, wiping down surfaces, and, of course, he poured himself a small drink and swallowed it with his back to Farrell. Farrell sat in a booth, looked at his watch, then he touched the texture of the cloth on the table. It was a cool, soothing place. A glass of beer sat on the table, the fluid as golden as a sunset over a wheat field, its head dreamily white, like a bride's veil.

"What's the rush?" said Shirushi. "You're calling me every day."

"You've got to listen," said Farrell. "There isn't a lot of time. I want your advice, but there's something else."

Shirushi wore a silk dress today.

"Remember you asked me to give you something? Do you want it?" he said.

"Sure, does a bear do it in the woods, quack, quack, quack. . . . Yeah. What is it?"

She signaled a waiter He came over and she asked for a bottle of water.

"Gas or flat," he said.

"Flat," she said. Then she turned to Farrell.

"So?" she said.

Careful, careful. Get her to do this, but don't get too close. . . .

"There's a man in the Brooklyn Bridge motel in Manhattan Beach ..."

"I know about him. We talked about him before," said Shirushi.

"You need to have someone follow him. It's got to be today."

"Why do we follow him?"

Farrell shook his head.

"He'll probably go out along Mulholland toward Malibu. He'll probably go into the brush some place along the line. I think if you are careful you will find something interesting."

"And when is this going to happen?" she said.

"Probably between rush hour and dusk," said Farrell. "Make the call. Will you?"

"He's got a bracelet on his ankle," said Shirushi. "What's the big deal?"

"I wouldn't depend on that," said Farrell.

She kept her eyes on him as she thought it over. Time is money, and the department had budget difficulties. Then she might be asked where she found out about this, whatever it was. A confidential informant, right?

Shirushi made a call, spoke for a while, waited for a call back, then went through the same details, sipping at her flat water. Then she hung up.

"You better be right about this," she said. "About him not wearing a bracelet."

"Oh, I'm right," he said.

"You don't sound glad?" she said.

He shrugged.

"Being right and being glad aren't always the same," he said.

"Uh-oh," she said. "You're splitting hairs. Got to be something going on here."

"Just between us, right?" said Farrell.

"Up to a point," she said. "I wonder if this has anything to do with the girls Jerry Macaulay says you were asking about, Portia and her friend, Charlene ... her last name escapes me, do you know what it is?"

"Klauski," Farrell said.

"They were picked up for shoplifting, and, as you know, they have a record for this and that, and so we were thinking that maybe a little time in the Youth Authority might do them some good, but I'm not so sure about that. And so, they said that they had something they could tell us about, you know, the movie business, but they had to think about it, and since they had a cheap lawyer, and since we were curious and since we thought we could wait, naturally we let them go."

She took another sip.

"This is about something else," said Farrell. "Not them. They're going to be in a movie."

"No kidding," she said.

"This is something else," said Farrell.

"You want to know the secret of police work? I told you once. You don't chase someone down. You just wait for them to do the same stupid thing a second or a third time ..."

He took a drink of the cold beer. If he could only live that way for a while, a cold drink in a quiet bar in the late afternoon. With Rose Marie smiling on the other side of the table that was covered with a linen cloth.

"So, you said something on the phone about asking my advice," she said.

"Yes," said Farrell. "Which is the worst rap? Moving a body a great distance and trying to make sure it is never found, or if you just left it close to where something happened ..."

"Something?" she said.

"Please," he said.

"I warned you," she said. "Looks like you got yourself into a perfect position. It reminds me of the Inquisition. They had a piece of interrogation equipment, a box, and if you were being interrogated, they put you in the box. The sides could be adjusted so you couldn't stand up and you couldn't sit down."

"Yeah," Farrell said. "Sounds familiar, you know, when you are confined."

"If a body was left near where *something happened*," she said. "A good defense lawyer could make all kinds of excuses. Panic. Stupidity. Temporary insanity. But if someone made the effort to hide it, really hide it, then you have a rock-ribbed murder one item."

Her hair shined even in the dim light of the bar. Black hair with silver streaks.

"So, there it is," she said. "The girls, like all girls or a lot of girls, want to be in the movies. And you say that's separate from this. All right. Okay. I'm not saying that you have anything to do with them, aside from asking about them."

"I ask about all kinds of people," Farrell said. He shrugged. What's the big deal?

"Something about you makes me uneasy," she said. "Give me a little more."

"I think keeping an eye this afternoon on western Mulholland is a good idea. But you don't have much time. You really don't."

"We'll get around to it," she said. "Is that all?"

He nodded.

"All right," she said. "You've got my cell and my landline, right?"

"Yes," he said.

"Just in case something else comes up," she said.

She winked at him, a frank, knowledgeable blink, and then that dangerous smile.

20

THE BEST TIME TO GATHER the girl, Farrell thought, if he was going to take Shirushi's advice to make this look as bad as possible, was in that first blue light of dawn. Rose Marie was at her window when Farrell came out of his house in the first dim light, when shapes were emerging from the dark. She didn't wave. Farrell thought, Don't underestimate me. Those of us down here in the Ninth Circle know a thing or two.

He had no idea what had happened the previous afternoon when Shirushi or her associates had followed Karicek to the Alaskan girl. He hoped this had happened, but it was always difficult to know how seriously a cop took some advice. He was sure of one thing. Karicek would have taken the girl a long way from Terry's house. In fact, he knew, or suspected that this was so, if only because he had searched and found nothing close by. At least he wasn't worried about being on Mulholland. Shirushi would have been miles away the day before, closer to the beach. There was no reason for her to be around this morning. Is that right? he thought. Well, this was one way to find out.

On Mulholland the dawn came with that first blue on the verge of gray, like a medical symptom, and then the stars or planets begin to fade, and then shapes of things, houses, trees, stones at the side of the road, telephone poles, wires showed themselves, as though they had been produced in the dark. Some people were up early, but not many, and they were visible on Mulholland because they had their headlights on. In the Camry glove box sat some protein bars that came from the economy size box at Coin-A-Matic. Four bottles of water were in the back seat, which he thought should be enough even for the desert.

The dirt next to the brush was still damp with dew, and the car stopped with a softness, a delicacy in that damp loam. The lights of the Valley were fading too, not quite as festive at this hour as they usually were, like those for some a failing amusement park. The trunk lid just rested on the sill of the body of the car so that it appeared like it was closed. The Department of Water and Power sign was still on the dashboard, but it was still invisible, given the light. Maybe someone who stopped would think that those Department of Water and Power guys were hard workers. The last two stars, above the smoky air, became more gray. Over the Ventura Freeway a long line of smoke was beginning to form.

When any large change takes place, or at the beginning of action, a clarifying moment appears, and Farrell knew this was the case, if only because he faced nothing but anxious uncertainty, delusion, and personal static, as though what he wanted was only a matter of electricity. Still, vengeance has an icy clarity.

The snakes would probably be out early, since they had waited all night for the prey to begin to move. And the best time for them was before the afternoon, or before the strong light, when they could sun themselves in the dappled shade. They were pit vipers, which meant that they hunted by looking for heat, and Farrell wondered if they could sense the temperature of his skin through his boots and jeans. Of course, they could.

The British girl had not been disturbed, at least as far as he could tell. No obvious tearing of flesh, no small nibbling, no work of coyotes. Some insects had made a path, like a river seen from the air, from the obscurity of the brush to where the girl was. If she had been farther from the road, maybe the animals might have done their work, but the passing of the cars, the people who came to park here at night, the cars during the day, had probably scared them away. Hawks, at least, wanted recently killed animals.

Farrell didn't know how many days the girl had been here, but she wasn't in the horrific condition he had been afraid of. Terry had kept her on ice for a while. Still, did Catherine know what the darkness really was, or how it could be seen after eight days, or so, when the British girl's skin would turn red and blistered. Or that the underworld claimed by its horrors, by the colors, the blisters and a vile tug downward, what it did when it was finally in charge. The presence, the decay came to Farrell as a touch, a hint of all that was most horrifying. Catherine, he thought, Catherine.

The latex gloves had the unseemly touch of a condom. A real body bag would have been better, since here she would have to be slipped into the open end of the construction bag without a zipper to close it up. But she was small and light, and the easiest way was to arrange her along the fall line of the hillslope, head at the bottom, and put the mouth of the bag under her and then wiggle it toward her feet. It was impossible to pretend there was no odor in the air, and so the best thing was to give up and just pull the bag to her feet and tie the ends. The brush rustled as Farrell got it close to the road, on the shoulder.

The unlatched trunk opened with a sigh. The bag went in. Farrell made sure the trunk was locked. A piece of manzanita was at the side of the road and he used it to sweep out the tracks before he threw it into the canyon. The limb of manzanita, with its small leaves, appeared like a dark bird as it spun over the steep hillside. He started the engine, went up to Laurel Canyon, and turned right. It would take him, depending on traffic, a couple of hours get to the Mojave Desert.

He had driven through these places many times, Fontana, Victorville, and the rest. The towns were places he had been glad to avoid right from the first times when he had come here as a teenager. The reasons were obvious, the clutter, the sense that at a stoplight it wouldn't take much to start a fight, or the fact that Fontana was a sort of hometown to the Hells Angels. The town wasn't obviously that rough, although it had a hint of the ominous, and something else, too, which was harder to invoke but still there. The place perfectly melded the possibilities of malice since it was built on the edge of a desert, where the essential hostility of the landscape was just below one's awareness. Still, a ghost of that hostility lingered. When people in Ohio thought of California, they weren't thinking of Fontana.

It happened in Barstow. Even though the Camry got good mileage, it needed gas, and so on the outskirts of Barstow Farrell stopped at a house that had been converted into a gas station and restaurant. Two gasoline pumps sat out front. It had a lunch counter that served bacon cheeseburgers, fries cooked in suet, and chili made from poached venison that was advertised as beef.

The sign in front said, "Black's Gas N Market, cold beer, water, Coke, Mountain Dew, Sandwich Meat, Lunch Counter, last gas for a hundred miles." The sign looked like it had been painted by a kid, just someone trying to help out around a store at the edge of the desert.

The dust of the parking lot blew behind Farrell, like a cloud of ill will. The nozzle of the pump went into the gas tank, and the sky was so haunting in its white-blue indifference as to make Farrell feel suspended. The pump ran very slowly, as though out here in the heat, everything was careful.

Next to the door of Black's, a woman tipped a chair back. She kept her eyes on the car, on the slowly moving numbers of the pump, and on Farrell. Would she remember him, be able to describe the man who stopped to get gas?

He was never sure why people trusted him at first glance. Maybe it was that he looked a little like a character actor, one of those guys who played a member of the platoon that was about to get wiped out, and maybe it was that he had his hair cut a little like a Navy SEAL, wore jeans, had that smile, white teeth, and greenish eyes the color of money. The woman wore jeans, too, a flannel shirt, which should have tipped him off, since it was the wrong thing to wear here, in the desert. She was blond, her hair streaked, uncombed, and while she was very attractive, she was so thin it looked to Farrell that meth might have had something to do with it. Or Molly. It was hard to tell, but she had a hard beauty, a smile that was a little too ready and a little too false. Farrell wanted to fill the tank and get away. The less anyone saw the better.

"Hi," she said. The knob of the door of Black's was hot enough to make popcorn.

"Hi," he said, looking down and away.

"Getting hot, huh?"

She put a hand through her thick hair, and her scent suggested she hadn't had a shower in a couple of days.

"Which way are you going?" she said.

"East."

"Away from LA," she said. "That's for the best I guess."

She had her hands in her pockets and glanced up the road, which now began to shimmer in the heat, and the mirages there, those lakes of silver, began to reflect the mountains in the distance, which seemed Martian.

The woman behind the counter said, "Credit card or cash?"

"Cash," Farrell said.

Farrell put the precise amount on the counter, down to the penny. Was that a mistake? Wasn't it more likely that someone would remember a man who had quarters, dimes, nickels?

He kept his face down.

"That woman outside wants a ride," said the cashier. "I'd leave her alone."

"Why?" he said.

"Call it woman's intuition," said the cashier. "Good luck. A lot of hot, empty country where you're going." She looked out the window at the blacktop that ran into the desert. "You want a water bag?"

"I don't think so."

"Well, you can't say you weren't warned," she said.

On the porch the hair of the woman was so tangled it was beginning to look like dreads.

"Everything come out all right?" she said.

"Yes," he said.

"All cleaned up? Hands washed?"

The woman stood up. She was tall and very thin. Meth for sure, he thought. She obviously had something to offer, to tell, to say, and Farrell was willing to bet it was more intricate than the stories of most women who end up on the front porch of a desert store that was getting ready to go under. Soon, a BP would take over with a mini-mart and microwave burritos. No lunch counter with burgers and fries.

"Can you do me a favor?" she said.

"I'm in a hurry," he said.

"I won't slow you down. And I don't take up much space," said the woman.

"Look . . ."

"No, *you* look," she said. She stepped closer, and brought him into her fragrance. "Don't you want me to be nice?"

"Sure," he said. He kept his face toward the distant mountains. "But I'm in a h-h-hurry . . ."

"Me, too," said the woman. "That gives us something in common. And why do you keep looking away. Don't you want me to remember you?"

The air still had some dust that the car had brought up to the pumps. A fragrance of the desert lingered, like a desiccant that would leach moisture out of any living thing it touched. The door of the Camry opened with a reassuring click, the precision of the engineering, the nature of the metal seeming at odds with the desolation of the store, the landscape, the porch. The steering wheel was already hot, and the key in the ignition was, too. He wasn't even surprised, really, when the woman from the porch opened the passenger's door and got in.

"Look," he said.

"My name is Ellen."

"Ellen," he said.

"Yeah," she said. "Sort of nice, don't you think, like a farm wife?"

He didn't want to stare, but the pistol she had was a .38, snub nosed, a revolver, some of the bluing gone, although the hammer was pulled back.

"You know," he said. "I've never been carjacked before."

"There's a first time for everything," she said. "And, you know, a last time, too."

"You mean like getting killed," he said.

"Well," she said. "At least you aren't stupid. Yeah. There's a last time, too."

"You don't know what you're getting into," he said. "I'd like to warn you. I really would."

"You're warning *me*," she said. "What have you been smoking?"

"I could just sit here. And wait you out. That is, I could make you shoot me right here, and I don't think you want to do that."

"No," she said. "I want you to drive me for a while."

"But if I don't," he said. "You've got to shoot me. Or get out. They both have dangers."

"You know," she said. "You don't rattle very easily, do you? Most guys start sweating bullets in circumstances like this. What do you do for a living?"

"It doesn't matter," he said.

"Start the engine," she said.

He thought what she would look like if he just let her have the car, and she got stopped by the cops. When they opened the trunk, she'd say, "Oh, That. That. Well. Let me explain . . ."

Too bad the car was registered to him.

"I think you are making a m-m-mistake," he said.

"Funny," she said. "Mostly the guys I deal with say just do this, take off your panties, and I promise you everything will be all right . . . but you don't do that. What gives?"

"I've got five hundred dollars in cash," he said.

"Give it to me," she said.

It was folded over in the front pocket of his shirt so there would be no need to open a wallet where a driver's license was visible. He reached the money with two fingers, took it out, and passed it over.

"That's a lot of meth," he said.

"Not for me," she said. "Start the car. Drive."

"Where?" he said.

"Into the desert. I don't care where, really. I just got to think a little."

"I was considering the Yarrow Ravine," he said.

"Where the rattlesnakes are? What were you going up there for?"

"A picnic," he said.

"Yeah," she said. "Where's your basket?"

He took one of the energy bars from his pocket.

"Everything is smaller these days," he said. "Even picnics. I just walk around, think things over, you know, take a little walkabout."

"Go on," said Ellen. "You know what? I should shoot that place up, Black's. They wouldn't even let me use the bathroom. Because I didn't buy something. So, fuck them."

"Sure," he said.

"Well?" she said. "Are we going to settle this here or are we going to take a drive? And you don't want a picnic. You want privacy. So, we have something in common, right?"

"So how did you end up sitting on a porch?"

"Wow," she said. "You must be a cop or something. Get them talking, right? Isn't that what the hostage negotiators do?"

"I'm not a cop," he said.

"No," she said. "I bet you're something worse."

He glanced at the pistol and thought, Oh, my dear Ellen, have you made a mistake.

The road was just two-lane blacktop, but the car still left a cloud of dust behind, as though it was vanishing into the dry, vicious air of the desert.

Ellen looked in the glove box, but only found the owner's manual, registration, which she looked at for a moment, still keeping that pistol in her lap, and said, "Laurel Canyon. So, what are you, a movie star?"

"No."

She picked up the iPad, turned it on, pulled up the pictures. Catherine, Jack, Ann, Gerry.

"Who are these?" she said.

"Kids," he said.

"They aren't looking too good," she said. "A little sickly."

He looked right into her eyes.

"Jesus," she said. "What's with that look? Why if I didn't know better, I'd be afraid."

She turned off the iPad and put it away.

It wouldn't be good for her to take the car, since when it ran out of gas, he thought, or she left it someplace, the trunk was going to be opened. And it wouldn't be good to have any trouble with her anyplace where someone might call the cops. It wouldn't be good if she left him at the side of the road where someone might ask what the hell he was doing on a road in the Mojave Desert. Where was justice, that long dismissed item?

"Something smells a little funny," she said.

"We must have passed something d-d-dead at the side of the road."

"Yeah," she said. "I guess."

"So, where do you want to go?" he said. "Maybe we can work something out?"

"Yeah," she said. "Like what?"

"The first thing you can do is to put the hammer down on that," he said. He gestured to the pistol. "And when you do, point it out the window."

She put it down.

"Don't think I won't use it," she said. "Don't think it for a minute. So, what's eating at you?"

"Me?" he said. "Nothing."

"Tell me another." She swallowed. "You're heartsick."

"I didn't know I had one," he said.

"Don't be cute," she said. "I've had it up to here with cute."

The desert landscape slipped by, so gray and brown, so flat, so desolate as to make the occasional Joshua tree look good. Or vital.

"I'm trying to come up with a way that you don't have to use that pistol, you get where you want to go, and I keep my car. You've got five hundred dollars."

"That's a start," she said.

"Here," he said. The pillbox sat in his hand, the one with Botticelli's Venus on it. She opened it, took a Klonopin, and swallowed it dry.

"So," she said. "You sound like you are selling me a life insurance policy."

If you only knew.

"I do have a problem," he said.

"I believe you," she said. "I don't know why, but I do." She handled the pistol. "Have we met before?"

"I don't think so," he said. "So, what do you want? No lies. That's the ground rule."

She stared straight ahead.

"I bet you do all right with women," she said.

"Not really," he said.

"Bullshit," she said. "I'd fuck you right now."

"Before you kill me?" he said. "Sort of a black widow?"

"I guess that would depend," she said. She laughed at the notion.

"How did you come to be sitting on that porch back there?"

"Lying men, cheap bosses, women who pretended to be friends and weren't, and some screwy ideas about coming to California. The oldest story there is. Does that do it? I mean, what are the odds I had in Plymouth, New Hampshire?"

"Better than this," he said.

"I'm trying to figure that out," she said.

That desert landscape, so dry, so threatening, slid by.

"I got to take a leak," she said. "Black wouldn't let me use the bathroom. Like I had some venereal disease I was going to leave on the toilet."

"I'll stop farther up," he said. "You can take the keys and go back into the bushes away from the road."

"Shit," she said.

"So, tell me," he said.

"You really have a nice voice, you know that?" she said.

If I could just live up to it, he thought.

"I grew up in New Hampshire," she said. "I was young. Sixteen. I looked good. I came out here and I thought I was going to get in the movies. How fucking dumb. You know, girls still think that, or did fifteen years ago. How old do you think I am?"

He thought she looked forty, but he said, "Thirty-five."

"Thirty," she said. "Life out here can be hard."

She glanced over at him.

"So, you know what?" she said. "I couldn't get anywhere. Nowhere. Until I met a young actor, you know, he had some parts, and I let him sleep with me and then I threatened him with going to the cops, since I was sixteen. That's all he needed. A rape charge."

"I guess that happens," he said.

"Not as many charges as there should be," she said.

I'm with you there, he thought.

"So, you know what happened?" said Ellen.

He drove through that landscape, which was an off-brown, marked by gullies and plants that looked like they should be dead but through some miracle weren't.

"S-s-some guy showed up, right?" he said.

"Yeah," said Ellen. "And when he was done with me, I was lucky not to be in jail."

"All in hints about what might happen, right?" he said.

"That's right," she said. "But I had some fun. You know, parties, and I even got flown to Europe, Paris, you ever been to Paris? Why, I drank champagne, watched the dawn from a bridge over the Seine. It was a good time. But soon, I was charging money."

"A girl's got to eat," he said.

"Yeah," said Ellen. "But you meet some people that aren't the kind you want to bring home to mom and dad."

"I know," he said.

"It sort of spirals down," said Ellen. "It was the Russians who scared me. That's why I was on that porch. I just want to get back to New Hampshire."

"They were getting ready to hire you out as a dump girl," he said. "Right?"

Ellen closed her eyes.

"Yeah," she said. "Paid to be beaten. What are you, psychic?"

"No," he said.

"So, what are we going to do?" she said.

"I've got a problem. If you take this car, you are going to have a problem, too."

"So?" she said.

"Open the glove box. There's a little door at the top. Open it."

She reached in, pulled it down. Five thousand dollars fell out.

"Consider this your lucky day," he said. "Take it."

She sat for a while with the money in her lap. Then she flipped the edge of the bills, like someone playing with a deck of cards. The Martian landscape rolled by.

"I got to pee," she said.

The Camry stopped in a cloud of dust on the shoulder of the desert.

"Me, too," he said.

She took the keys from the ignition, put them her pocket, and took the money, too. The door opened and the sage-scented air of the desert came in.

"Do it in front of the car," she said. "I'll be right over there."

She walked to the side of the road and then into that scrub. Outside, in that dust, it was possible that a buzzing rattle would begin as she squatted in the half shade of a Joshua tree. That's all he needed. But only the hissing of the wind came from the brush. There were dying languages of native people that had a windy sibilance ... the sound of wind moving across sand.

He pretended to pee in front of the hood, then reached down, took the extra key, and got in the car, locked the doors, started the engine and took off, running it up to seventy-five. In the rearview Ellen stood at the side of the road. Then she turned toward the scrub and threw the pistol into it, the thing twirling like some awkward, extinct bird. She stood at the side of the road, as still as a mannequin. She must have thought, What the fuck had happened?

Someone would pick her up, and she could keep going east. That was the best thing. New Hampshire, Vermont, Upstate New York ... maybe she'd have a chance. You dumb fucking Santa Claus, he thought. It gave him some relief not to have to think about how Terry would have used Ellen, years ago, if he had had the chance.

People always talk about rebirth as a pleasant thing, but what if it isn't, what if it is a kind of horror? You have to consider where you have been.

The desert air appeared in that ominous shimmer, that quivering sky that had a suggestion of all the heat of error, of folly, of delusion, of everything he had turned against but was unsure how to avoid.

The black birds, like checks in the sky, circled in that silver so keen and shiny as to seem more icy than hot. Sure, tell me about rebirth, he thought.

Yarrow Ravine was about ten miles along the road. The sign at the turn looked as though it had been sandblasted so that the letters on it, above the cartoon of a rattlesnake, appeared to be fading, and so was the yellow background that now looked like jaundiced fog. The sign read: RATTLESNAKE PRESERVE. DO NOT TANTALIZE THE SNAKES.

People still came here to see a snake or to catch one even though it was illegal, but mostly people left this part of the desert alone. The road wasn't that different from some of the others off the blacktop, just a dirt track with arroyos and scrub, mountains in the distance. The Camry left a long cloud of dust, as though it were some kind of exhaust from a locomotive. Even with the dust, the stink still came into the car. The heat, or maybe it was just the sun pounding on the trunk of the car, made the odor worse. The road went straight for four or five miles, and it kept going until it got to the foothills with their long, tornado-shaped gullies that began at the top of a hill as a little seam but that got wider, more funnel-like and deeper as they went downhill.

Every now and then, as hard as it was to believe, a cloudburst took place here, and then the desert bloomed, green as jade and more vital, too, but it didn't last long. At the end of that long straight section of road, it turned to the left, toward a divide between one set of foothills and another, and in the space between them some willows grew, or what looked like willows.

If Shirushi was right, the more cunning, the more thinking that went into this, the worse it would be for the man who paid the price for what happened to the British girl. Mostly, though, he could depend on that repetitive, anonymous, indistinct landscape, the dirt itself seeming venomous, and, in fact, it was, if you were out here long enough without water. The sun that had been high when he had been at the store was beginning to move to the west. The right place would have absolutely no path, no sign of anyone walking, no trail markers, nothing. Or, with one keen marker. One telltale mark on the landscape. A Joshua tree with a blaze, a rock that looked like Abraham Lincoln's nose. . . .

The place was a couple of miles up from the turn, and as Farrell got out, a bank of misty air moved over the sun, and while dusk would come sooner, it meant something else, too. Snakes hated direct sunlight, since it kills them. They liked spotted shade, half overcast days, warmth but not the hard-hitting sunlight.

The direction Farrell had come from showed no signs of dust. Just that frank, empty air. This was another reason he had driven up here, since the dust would show, with at least fifteen minutes warning that someone was coming this way, but then, as far as Farrell knew, some jackass with an instinct for a thrill was backpacking here, in the hills or close to the willows.

He stood at the side of the car. No breeze, no movement, nothing but that forbidding landscape, which, of course, seemed worse than usual.

His watch showed 1:00 p.m. Somehow it had taken a lot longer to get out here than he thought, but that was all right. If he did this quickly he could be back in LA before dusk.

The odor wasn't as bad as it could have been if she'd been out in the brush this whole time, but it was there. It wasn't something smelled, but felt in the chest.

He took the shovel from the trunk. He didn't want to give a chance to the coyotes, small mammals, even wild dogs that had escaped from Fontana and other towns out here, not to mention carrion eating birds. He didn't want that. The identification had to be complete. Farrell, after all, was going to leave proof.

The wind of that dead language, that native dialect with the hiss of air over sand said, "Blessed is the man that heareth me, watching daily at my gates, waiting at the posts of my doors . . ." And what could he hear now that he watched the landscape for any movement, and what would give a blessing? He kneeled in the shade of the car, closed his eyes, and thought, Oh, if I could only hear you. If I could only have listened to what you wanted when you got on that plane from London. The usual sad dreams, he guessed. Is that what he heard? It must have been a vision of beauty, of power, of success.

Farrell put on the latex gloves and picked up the bag by its knotted end, the edges bound together in a sloppy, but still tight, knot. He wanted to drag it, but that would just leave marks, even out here, and so he carried the bag like a grotesque pietà. The more devious, the worse, said Shirushi. "Blessed is the man that heareth me . . ." He shook his head, and as the weight, which was really not much, got heavier, as though the bag had a moral weight that was far, far heavier than any object subject to the earth's gravity, he went on walking although he glanced at the sun, just to make sure he knew how he would get back. Oh, he thought, I hear you, but it is too late. Far too late. But, he thought, I can make you a promise now.

If he could have only found her before this mess, before this miasma of LA got her. God knows it wasn't her fault that the lies assholes tell were beginning to seem like truth. I hear you, he thought, but he knew the truth was her weight in his arms, and not just the physical part.

He untied the top of the bag, stepped back, and pulled the corners at the bottom so that she was exposed. The buzzing began then, and so he stood still, hands on the bag. That was one of the difficulties of this particular sound. It was hard to tell precisely where it was coming from, and he wondered if that was part of its viciousness, that you would try to get away, but instead stepped on the snake you wanted to avoid. The clouds spread their darkness, and the gray shadow now covered him, the bag and the snake.

The immensities of the instant, and the scale of the malignant that existed here was evident to no one but him: What moral purity, what chance for the most profound decency had been squandered in all this?

He dug a quick, shallow trench, the perfect example of what Shirushi would have thought was the worst. The desire to conceal, but with a keen clumsiness.

The snake didn't bite him. For Farrell its presence, its curious sense of observing, was worse than a bite, even though Farrell had seen what a bite did. If someone was bitten, the venom digested the flesh, and in doing so it left patches that appeared to be encrusted with rubies in a clear but drying secretion. Lymph fluid, dissolving tissue? Something like that.

A bite, at least, was a definite action. The horror of the snake's constant, sliding presence was an accumulation of all those items that lurked in the shadows, the murder, cruelty, deviousness, corruption, everything that now seemed to exist as an invisible, inescapable cloud. The snake was a reminder of folly, of the gravity of the worst of events, of the things that had seeped into Farrell's awareness of himself and from which he was almost panicky in his desire to escape.

The beauty of the time the snakes had spent here was in how difficult it was to spot one, but after fifteen minutes, the thing was obviously curled in the dusty shrub. The markings on the back were regular, almost like a fractal, one segmented pattern, oval and yet edged with marks like the teeth of a saw, one after another, and while it was curled, as though to strike, it had stopped making that noise. He guessed the bag, warmed by the sun, would attract the snake. They hunted by the little pits beneath their eyes, which were sensitive to heat. Its head went first, flowing away from the coil of its body, and then the entire thing moved along, not undulating from side to side like a sidewinder, but got along with a locomotion that was almost otherworldly. It made no noise. It hardly left much of a track, and as it turned its head toward Farrell, it seemed to dismiss him with such contempt as to leave him doubting whether he existed, or maybe he was so filled with self-loathing and the desire to be someplace else that it was indistinguishable from fear. Blessed is the man that heareth me, watching daily at my gates, waiting at the posts of my doors. Can you hear me, Catherine? Am I doing the right thing?

She had slipped out of the bag, which he had discarded as though it was the flag of the worst thing imaginable. Her clothes were a little more dirty, but still the same: a tank top, a vest, dark jeans, and those running shoes with the holes along the side of the sole. The snake flowed along, as though keeping him company. The pale light left him with more of that sense of not existing at all, and he wondered if, after all these years, he had finally gotten in over his head, not in the ability to fix things, but in the ability to still exist.

He had come to a sort of vaporization of what he thought he had been, which was a competent man who took care of hypocritical nonsense, and who meant well in a tough world. But it always led somewhere to that ultimate darkness. Always. Now, for an instant, he had a yearning for some clean, infinitely suffering, infinitely loving thing.

The shadows of the clouds were like smoke from the underworld, at once gray and filled with menace. And that gray presence had something new, or something he had to face. How, for instance, does it play out? How do you see into the future, and just how will justice be done? Or will vengeance devour its own? Was he one of justice's own?

The Italian toothbrush was still in the ziplock bag, and Farrell brought it from the glove box of the car. The British girl had stolen it, he guessed, as an elegant souvenir. Here, thought Farrell, as he put the brush, bristles first, into the side of her running shoes, Here's a souvenir. When she was found, the question would be, What was she trying to say? Why did she have this stylish item, this thing that could appear in an advertisement in *Vogue*? He pushed the tooth-brush down so it appeared she was hiding it, or so that no one would know she had it.

Above him were three stones, about ten feet tall, each shaped like a football on end, and on each side there were three Joshua trees. And, to his surprise, someone had left a Willys Jeep, blistered with rust, the windows cracked like an infinite number of spider webs. Those stones, he thought, were good enough landmarks, along with the Jeep.

"Blessed is the man that heareth me . . ."

At the car he found a piece of tumbleweed, the brushy globe of it about the size of a beach balloon. It was handy to wipe out where he had walked, and as much of the tire tracks as possible, although there wasn't much of that. The surface here, for a short distance, was hard as a dry lake. Then he brushed back to the side of the car and threw it away. Yes, he could depend on that harshness.

He considered that snake as it had flowed along, as it had glanced at him, and then slid away. He'd be back in LA before dark.

21

THE SHADOWS OF EARLY EVENING in front of Farrell's house were soft, a little gray, the color of a sweatshirt. As he waited at the wheel of the car, the dirt on his hands, the scent of the desert constant, like a dust storm, his fatigue now a pressure, too, as in an airplane that is going down a runway for takeoff. Farrell wanted to open the door of the car, to go into his house and take a bath, but he sat there instead. Maybe, he thought, I am dehydrated. Yeah, sure.

Rose Marie tapped on the window of the driver's side. She stood in a light that makes for a dreamy quality, always seductive, no matter what you have seen.

"Look what the cat dragged in," she said.

"I had to take a drive," he said.

"A drive?" she said. "It must have been one hell of a drive."

"I'll snap out of it," he said.

"You'll snap out of it," she said. "I hope."

The leaves of the hedge that made a wall between the two houses and the road had that golden look, as though each leaf had been dipped in gilt, and the effect was a charm that mesmerized Farrell, since he was so tired as to want to take something from the light.

"How much trouble are you really in?" she said. "No lies."

No lies.

"You remember my talk with Catherine?"

"Yes," she said. "And so now you're like this. Angry. No, infuriated."

"I don't know," he said.

"Well, I do. Look. Look in the rearview mirror."

If only I could, he thought. And I'm not even done. Not yet.

A green Morgan car, with a belt to hold the hood shut, pulled up and parked in front of Rose Marie's house.

"That's my ex-boyfriend. He'll say he came to get the snake," she said.

Farrell finally got out of the car.

"A handsome guy," he said. "He should be in the movies. But you say he's an academic."

A man got out of the green car. He was in his late thirties with dark hair in which there was some gray, a widow's peak, and a thin build. For all his good looks, he had a chameleon quality, though his expression wasn't a blank. He looked like he smelled something he didn't like or as if he had stepped in dog shit. Irritated, but not knowing what to do.

"So," he said to Rose Marie. "This is where you ended up?"

"That's right," she said.

"You threatened to go, but I never believed you," he said. "So, I'm going to give you one more chance."

"Excuse me," Farrell said to Rose Marie. "Maybe I better go . . . I've got to make a call."

"No," she said. "I don't have any secrets. This is Andris Dolman. We used to live together. When he wasn't in Timbuktu."

"So, that's the problem?" Andris said.

"No," she said. "That's not the problem."

"So what is? And don't say you wouldn't understand."

"You wouldn't understand," she said.

"Oh, fuck, you're doing that thing again," he said. "Stop it. You can come home if you want."

"This is home," she said.

"Well, well," he said. He had the perfect air of a man who had never been dumped and was trying to understand what it really felt like. The transformation from exquisite vanity to injured pride was perfect. He put his hands on his hips and looked at Rose Marie.

"All right," he said. "Give me the key to our apartment."

She took her key ring from her pocket, the keys making a domestic jingle as she looked for the right one, but Andris grabbed the ring, his hands shaking. She reached for it and he pushed her arm away.

With a jerk that even surprised Farrell, he took the key ring from Andris's hands.

"Which one is it?" said Farrell.

The hedge, the house, the cars all seemed to be getting brighter. Is that fury? thought Farrell. Is that why objects appeared bright to him, as though covered with a sheen? Does fury arrive like a chrome-tinted cloud?

"The one with Yale on it," said Rose Marie.

Farrell handed over the key from the Yale lock.

"So, who's this?" said Andris Dolman.

"A friend," she said.

Andris stepped closer to her.

"A friend," he said. "Looks like a very good friend."

He stepped a little closer yet.

"Where did you dig this one up?" said Andris Dolman.

"You don't have to be that way," said Rose Marie.

"Look," Farrell said to Rose Marie. "Maybe you want to talk this over without me around."

"No," she said. "I'm asking you to stay."

"What is this guy?" Dolman said.

"I wouldn't talk that way if I were you," Farrell said.

"Is that a warning?" he said. "It sounds like a warning."

"Let's be grown up," Farrell said. "Get in your car, take your key, and leave . . ."

"I bet you are some sort of cheap Hollywood parasite," he said.

"If I were you, I'd get in my car and go home . . ." Farrell said.

"Jesus," said Andris Dolman to Rose Marie. "I thought you had taste. And you end up with this?"

"What did you say?" said Farrell.

They were close enough so that the stuff Andris used on his hair, some kind of mousse, made a sickly perfume fog that Farrell stood in. It clashed with that lingering scent of the desert.

"Go home," said Rose Marie to Andris.

"And leave you with this bum?" he said.

"Don't call me that," Farrell said. "Don't . . ."

"Oh. I hit home. I see," he said.

"Don't call me a bum," Farrell said.

They stood in that fading light, which should have been soothing but now was tainted, ugly, and oppressive. A car went down the street, its tires hissing.

Rose Marie turned to Farrell, her expression now one of curiosity and the first awareness of fear. Not because of the presence of her ex-boyfriend, but because of something else here, some hint of violence on Farrell's part that left her hesitant, or just waiting in the way someone does when a fuse has been lighted. Farrell glanced at her.

"Don't," she said to Farrell. She shook her head.

He guessed she knew something was happening, but did she know what it really was? Did she know, or suspect, that Farrell had been able to keep everything under control? That he had been able to behave with restraint, but that now he was losing that? Did she know that, for him, for an instant, it was elation?

Did Rose Marie know that the British girl, the time spent searching along Mulholland, the resistance to the mess Farrell had found himself in was crystallizing into precisely what he had wanted to avoid? Is that what made her hesitate, the air of approaching violence? Or was it more than just the violence, which was a symptom, but the anger behind it, which now hung in the air like an invisible gas that changed everything?

Rose Marie put her hand to her mouth, as though surprised.

"Riffraff, low-rent scum," said Andris.

Maybe he had never had his nose broken, or his throat closed, so he didn't know what he was dealing with, thought Farrell. Farrell was letting go, and he knew it. What would be better than to break Andris's injured vanity?

Andris nodded, looked around, glanced at Rose Marie, and said, "Too bad. You were a nice piece."

Then he was sitting on the ground, on his rear end, his head against the side of his car. When Farrell hit Andris's throat, Andris had gasped and put his hands to his neck. He wasn't really hurt, or if so, it was that his vanity that had been injured.

Rose Marie's trembling hand was on Farrell's.

"That's enough," she said. "Please."

It was Andris's smirk, his simpering condescension that charged everything. Andris's hair was thick, and a handful of it made it easy for Farrell to turn him over. Andris tried to speak, but when he opened his mouth, Farrell shoved Andris's teeth against a wheel rim of that stupid car. Farrell stood on one foot, about to do it, to break the teeth by kicking Andris in the back of the head.

Even then, in the midst of it, Farrell sensed Rose Marie's horror. He wondered if she really understood the extent of his fury, or the fact that he might not be able to control it as he had before. Is that what left her with that expression of mystification and terror? Did she really understand just by the mood, the air of threat and violence?

Rose Marie kept her eyes on Farrell.

"No, no," she said.

"For two cents, I'd . . ." said Farrell. "I'd . . ."

His hands were trembling as though he had been in an automobile accident.

Farrell stepped back, still trembling, aware that he was confusing one thing with another. What about the British girl? What about her? Wasn't that the problem?

Rose Marie went on staring, amazed, at Farrell. Andris Dolman stood up, not bothering to brush himself off, and as he stood, he wobbled a little.

"I'm sorry, I'm sorry, I'm sorry," said Andris Dolman.

"D-d-don't come back," said Farrell.

"I'm sorry," Andris Dolman said.

"Get in your car and get out of here," said Rose Marie. "What a stupid car."

"All right," he said. "I'm going to go."

"No, you aren't," said Rose Marie. "You're going to take your snake so you have no reason to come back."

She turned and went into the house. Andris Dolman and Farrell stood opposite each other, just staring, considering what could be done. Andris held his throat and made a sound when he tried to breathe like water first spurting out of a hose that has just been turned on. A wet, fast hush. Then Rose Marie came out of the house, carrying the habitat. The snake inside was coiled as always like a pile of small inner tubes.

"Open the door," she said to Andris Dolman.

The habitat went into the front seat. She slammed the door, then turned on her heel and walked away from the car. Andris got in behind the wheel, started the engine, never looking at either one of them, and then backed up, turned, and just before he went through the hedge, he flipped Rose Marie the finger.

Rose Marie put her hand on Farrell's forearm, just rested it there, and kept her eyes on the dust that lingered in break in the hedge.

"He shouldn't have called me a bum," Farrell said.

"I know, I know," she said.

She went on staring, as though the pieces of a puzzle were left on a table, and it would take a little time to put them together.

"Don't be angry," Farrell said.

"I don't know what to say," she said.

She shook her head.

"I need a moment to think," she said. She stood in the yard, seemingly calm, but considering that change in atmosphere, that miasma of threat, of violence, or worse, the anger behind it.

She looked at Farrell and said, "You're up to something that leaves you in a rage. You won't trust me. And I shouldn't be angry? Well, that's great. I take you to see the kids. I open my heart to you, I deal with your thugs coming around some sketchy business, and what I get from you is silence. You were ready to put Andris in a hospital. And I'm not supposed to be angry? Did you see what happened here?"

Farrell put out his hand, tried to take hers.

"I need to go back to being alone," she said.

"You mean that?" he said.

She looked back.

"Give it a little time," she said. "I don't want to mean it. You know that. But . . ." She gestured to the hillside, the sky as though the presence of Los Angeles was somehow part of the problem.

"Don't you see?" she said. "I don't know if I can live with this much anger."

Her fear stopped him and made him alert, as though he was listening for the beginning of an earthquake. Immobile, uncertain, only aware of some change.

Then she went into the house.

22

WAITING, AS FAR AS FARRELL was concerned, was a little like death, since, as he saw it, waiting was a sign of the absence of something that should be there. He considered Rose Marie and knew that he had already allowed his sense of himself to blend at the edges with some aspect of her, a smile, a touch, the time they'd spent together in bed, and that he was able to be a certain way when he was with her, but now that she seemed to be gone, that had vanished. So he was afraid that not only had he lost her, but also that he'd lost a part of himself he had grown to like. He wondered if it was the same for her. Waiting left him homesick for something that existed only when he was with her. If he had to say what his hope was, it would be that she knew what he was thinking.

She left her house and went to work. He picked some roses, wrapped them in newspaper, and left them on her step. When she came home, she picked them up, glanced in his direction, and went inside.

YouTube videos seemed to help Farrell with the waiting, or at least made the hours pass in a more invisible way. That's the thing about time, as it appeared to Farrell, slow when you want it to be fast, fast when you want it to be slow. And brooding is like being in a river, a black one to be sure, that always goes downhill.

The video he watched was of a whale on a beach in Oregon, filmed in the seventies. Too big to bury or to cart off. And someone had the idea of putting dynamite under the carcass and setting it off. Yes, thought Farrell, is that why I'm watching? Have I put dynamite under my own whale? What happens when it goes off?

* * *

At the Hollywood Bowl fountain, Braumberg was tired, his eyes filled with an expression that Farrell recognized. Braumberg's exhaustion was what saved him from terror. The fountain bubbled behind them.

Farrell said, "I need to know how many shooting days you have left."

"It's over," said Braumberg. "We're done. Or Terry's part is done."

"All right," said Farrell. "That's what I needed to know."

"You have no idea how brutal a shooting schedule. You have so many days, and that's it. What happens if you get cut off before you have enough to edit what you've shot?"

"But Terry's done?" said Farrell.

"Yes," said Braumberg.

He hesitated as he reached for Farrell's hand.

"I want to thank you for holding off on whatever you're going to do. I'm not going to ask, but I want to thank you. At least the picture is done."

Farrell nodded, as though he was looking at his last meal.

"But here's an odd thing," said Braumberg. "Maybe I am tired, but I don't think that's it. That girl, Portia Blanchard, you know who I mean?"

"How could I forget?" said Farrell.

"She is fantastic. We've seen the dailies and the camera loves her. She takes light in a way that is uncanny. People have come to look. We are going to use her in two new pictures. A bigger role. Just incredible. I've never seen anything like it. Enough to make me think of magic."

* * *

At the pastry shop, Du-par's in Studio City, Shirushi looked tired, too. She sat in her jeans and a short-sleeve shirt, her eyes bloodshot, her hands holding a cup of coffee.

"So," she said. "What gives?"

She said this with an air of mystification and keen suspicion, not to mention something like fear.

"This is between us," said Farrell. "Right?"

"Maybe," said Shirushi. "Maybe."

"I think you should look in the Mojave Desert. In a place called the Yarrow Ravine Rattlesnake Habitat."

"That could be a pretty big place," said Shirushi.

"At the end of the road there is a dry river."

"An arroyo," said Shirushi. "Is that what you mean?"

"Yeah. You go along that for exactly three tenths of a mile and you will find three stones, about ten feet high, that look like three perfect footballs. And next to them are three Joshua trees. About a hundred yards to the south, you will find some disturbed dirt. You know you are in the right place when you see an old Jeep. A Willys."

"No kidding," she said.

"There may be some personal items there. Like a toothbrush or something. I'd be sure to check it for DNA samples."

The display cabinet to the right of the booth where they sat was filled with bright raspberry tarts, cakes with white frosting and decorated with strawberries, and next to them were apple pies and then loaves of bread, a pile of croissants. Shirushi looked at them and then back at Farrell. He wondered just how much she would take before she arrested him, or if the attachment from the old days, when she arrested him for those motorcycles, still left them bound together. Like cousins, he hoped.

"All right," she said.

"How did you make out with Karicek?" said Farrell.

"We found his car, but not him. On Mulholland, halfway to Malibu. Still, we looked around and there was something in the bushes . . . is that what you thought?"

"Yes," said Farrell.

"That's what you thought. Young woman, just a girl really. Her jacket came from a store in Anchorage. So, we are in touch with the Alaskan state police. But if we don't get more, or if we don't pull in Karicek, we're going to have to get you involved. You understand?"

"Yes," said Farrell, "I do."

"A confidential source gets you only so far," said Shirushi.

She looked at him for a while.

"I'll be in touch," she said.

"Three stones, just like footballs. Along an arroyo. Three Joshua trees."

She nodded.

* * *

Farrell left more flowers on Rose Marie's door step, and when she came home, she picked them up and stood, her eyes on his house. Then she walked across the yard to Farrell's door and tapped, the sound at once inquisitive and delicate. So, he thought, maybe she felt it, too, that sense of missing a part of oneself. Maybe she had come to find it, that cloud of warm understanding, so hard to mention but so palpable in fact.

"I thought you weren't talking to me anymore," he said.

"The kids miss you," she said. "They ask about you."

"W-w-hat do you tell them?" he said.

"This and that," said Rose Marie.

"This and that," he said. "What kind of visitors are you inviting to talk to them?"

She blinked, then stood a little closer, as though comfort was so close she could almost step into it.

"A pro, a guy from the Harvard Medical School who works with terminal children came to talk to them and they told him to get fucked. I don't mean this figuratively, between you and me. I mean they said, 'Go fuck yourself.'"

"They meant something to me," Farrell said.

"They could tell," she said. "They're like tuning forks . . . you know, if you have an emotion, they sort of vibrate in harmony with it . . ."

"Oh, Jesus," said Farrell. "You are getting New Age on me."

"Well, you know what I mean," she said. "Can I come in?"

"I've been thinking about you," he said. "Details. It's hard to describe."

"I know," she said.

"Like being upstairs, under the skylight . . . and other things."

"So," she said. "You're working that end of things, huh? Upstairs? Gold sparkles, or something like them from my heels upward . . . and I thought I was over anything like that."

She brushed her hair back.

"Yes," she said. "There were other things."

She pushed against him.

"You know," said Rose Marie. "We have to talk first."

Farrell wondered if she knew that she seemed to be carrying with her a part of himself. Or maybe she had come to collect a part of herself. They stood next to each other.

"So, you're ready to hear it?" he said.

It all came out. Everything.

It took a while. The refrigerator hummed, the roof ticked as it cooled, and every now and then the kitchen faucet dripped, the water hitting the stainless-steel sink with a steady *tip tip tip*. Farrell didn't stutter. The details came out, one after another.

Rose Marie kept her eyes on his face, nodding a little from time to time. He finished and she went on looking at him.

"You think I am shocked by this? You think someone who lives in a world where kids die young is surprised by trouble like this. No. I'm not shocked and I am not surprised."

"But. . . ?" he said.

She went on looking at him. Then she closed her eyes as she thought it over, and when she opened them, she said, "I want one thing from you. Just one."

"All right," he said.

"I want you to realize how ugly this is and that it is going to stop. No more."

"You don't think I know how ugly this is?"

They looked at each other, the touch of their glances as soft as perfect understanding.

"Okay," she said. "Okay."

Then she sat down at the kitchen table. The iPad was there and she glanced at the YouTube video paused on the screen.

"So, you've got to wait," she said.

"That's the hard part," he said.

She tapped little arrow to make it play and the video started.

"What's that? Looks like a whale?" she said.

"Yeah. That's right," he said.

"Jesus, what's in those boxes?" she said.

"Dynamite," he said.

She glanced at him.

"Are you sure you're all right?"

"No. I am most definitely not sure," he said.

The people in the video put the dynamite as far under the whale as they could, and after that they ran a wire to a detonator, not one with a plunger but a little switch. The camera was behind the guy who turned the switch. Nothing happened. At least for about one heartbeat. In a starburst, or a harsh cloud of sand, the whale rose into the air, separated into chunks about the size of a VW Bug, and kept going up for a minute. When the pieces came down, they landed as though it was raining chunks of blubber, but so heavy as to flatten cars that had been parked along the beach by people who had wanted to see what was going to happen. The crowd moaned at first with a sensual delight at the explosion, and this moan changed into screams of horror as the pieces of the whale began to fall.

"How long is it going to take?" said Rose Marie. "How long are you going to have to wait?"

He shook his head.

"I wish I knew," he said.

Farrell moved the video back to the beginning. The whale appeared on the beach with its slick but scarred skin, as though you had shined your shoes and then hit them here and there with a hatchet.

The explosion under the whale had the shape of an enormous flak burst, a center with a dark, roundish bloom of violence. Farrell thought of the big bang. Was that the basic form in the universe, that bang, that explosion?

* * *

It took a couple weeks, but the guy with the gray beard and the bandana headband who delivered the *Los Angeles Times* in the truck with the cow horns, pulled into the yard and threw the papers, one for Farrell and one for Rose Marie. The man had a large joint in his ashtray, and after he threw the papers, he took a hit, then went out the break in the hedge. Rose Marie came over with the paper.

The headline read, "Terry Peregrine, star of the new blockbuster picture due in the fall, dies in single car, high speed accident at Cholame ..."

Rose Marie said, "Single car, huh? All by himself, right? Isn't that where James Dean died?"

"Yes," he said. "That's where he died."

Rose Marie put down the paper.

"I'd guess they questioned him about the British girl," Farrell said. "They must have come by his house to ask about her. Or maybe his lawyer started to work on the terms for giving himself up."

"To your cop friend?" said Rose Marie.

"For now she's a friend," he said. "At least it looks like it. She probably turned over the collar to Homicide. And then there are the cops in the Mojave. I'd guess the jurisdiction is a little unclear."

He turned the page of the paper, where there was a picture of Terry Peregrine. Young and attractive. It's a hard lesson, as the Buddhists say, to know the difference between how things appear and what they are.

"And the girls?" said Rose Marie.

"Braumberg saw the dailies. Portia is fantastic. The camera just loves her. He's going to use her in a new picture."

"And?" said Rose Marie.

"Terry's accident isn't going to hurt the picture. Not one bit. Romantic lead dies like one of the legends ..."

"Romance," said Rose Marie. "You just can't beat it."

"Let's h-h-ope," said Farrell.

"The hospital is going to get some money," she said. "I heard this producer is making a major contribution."

"I wonder how that happened," he said.

"Oh," she said. "I've got a pretty good idea."

"A little arm twisting at the right moment will do wonders."

"And what about the girls?"

"I guess any connection with Terry disappeared."

"You guess? And you talked to your pal, the cop, to go easy on the girls?" she said.

"What's to go easy about?" Farrell said. "What's a little shoplifting among friends?"

* * *

The next week the delivery guy with the red bandana and the joint the size of a small cigar pulled through the hedge and threw two copies of the paper into the yard.

Farrell had his spread on the table in his kitchen when Rose Marie came in.

"So," she said. "You've already seen it?"

The main headline, the one at the top said, "Wanted man found on the beach in Santa Monica." The sub head was, "Obvious suicide. Had been in water for weeks."

"I guess he had good reason," Rose Marie said. "After all, he was going to be sent to Pelican Bay."

"Have you ever seen Pelican Bay?" said Farrell.

"Just pictures," she said.

"The pictures don't do it justice," he said. "But I think it was more than that."

* * *

He met Shirushi at Pink's, and they sat at a picnic table in the back and ate chili dogs. Shirushi took small bites, and every time she did, she stopped to consider Farrell.

"I could ask about how you knew this shithead was going to look for the body of a girl from Alaska, but I'm not sure we'd get anyplace. Of course, I could arrest you, and cause trouble, but I'm not sure about that."

"That's right," said Farrell.

"Don't be too sure," she said. "So?"

"You want to have it tied together. Of course," said Farrell. "I understand."

"You better," she said.

Farrell took the postcard with the picture of the bear on it out of his pocket. He turned it over so that the message, with hearts and smiley faces for dots above the *i*'s, was visible. The handwriting had a hint of the pathological, of the devious and the stupid.

"Postmarked from Alaska," said Shirushi. "How do I know Terry sent him up there?"

Farrell took a credit card record and airline receipt from his pocket and pushed them over. The ticket to Anchorage on Terry's card was in Karicek's name. The date of the postmark was the same as the ticket.

"Well, well," she said. She put the credit card record and the airline's receipt for a ticket in her handbag, along with the postcard.

"You know," she said. "I could ask you where you got this, but it's all . . ."

"Moot," said Farrell.

"Moot?" she said. "What are you? Going to law school at night? Moot . . . well, here's what's moot. Terry's dead and so is his brother. There's nothing more, really."

Farrell reached over and picked up her hand and squeezed it.

"Stop being so sappy," she said. "I'm still not sure I'm going to leave you alone."

"I think you will," he said.

She finished the chili dog, rolled up the paper it had come in, and tossed it into a trash can with a flick of her wrist. Then she turned back to him.

"I told you once that the secret to good police work isn't always tracking someone down. You just wait for someone to do the same stupid thing again. So, I'll be watching you."

"Be my guest," he said.

"In your dreams," she said. "Pride goeth before a fall ..."

"Okay," he said.

"There's only one thing I don't get," she said. "Yeah, we should have gotten to Mulholland earlier to follow Karicek. We just got his car and the body of the girl, but not him. And so, I'm left wondering why would a guy like Karicek kill himself? Usually they hang on to the last minute."

"Maybe you should have got there earlier," said Farrell.

"Don't rub it in," she said. "Everyone makes mistakes."

"Pelican Bay is a bad place," said Farrell.

"Maybe," she said. "But I don't buy it."

"I wish I could tell you," said Farrell. "But I don't know."

* * *

In the evening, Farrell drove the Camry to Coin-A-Matic, parked, and went to the small door in the large one. He stood at the threshold and tried to imagine the whir of the fans built there that had made wind for movies. Then he went in, picked up his clipboard, and started going from one pile of boxes to another. The boxes were filled with small bags of Doritos, bacon-flavored potato chips, and candy bars. Next to these stood bottles of water in packs held together with shrink wrap. The light over the bench came down in a golden triangle, oddly domestic and commercial at the same time.

Nikolay and Pavel came in when he was examining his spreadsheet to see if they were losing money or not. It didn't really matter this month since Braumberg had him paid a lot of cash.

"Farrell," said Nikolay. "How are things?"

Farrell looked up from the spreadsheet. He was beginning to think that it would be a good idea to bring the Sig Sauer from his house and to leave it here. But, for now, he sat there, glancing from one of them to the other.

"You've come for your money?" said Farrell.

"No," said Nikolay.

"We saw in the paper about that guy. Karicek. The one you said was into auto parts. You remember that?"

"I remember," said Farrell.

"You should have come to us earlier," said Pavel. "We could have done some real business."

"What's real business?" said Farrell.

They stepped closer. Pavel sat down on a stool next to the bench with the golden cone of light and the tools on the wall.

"We never believed you about the auto parts," said Pavel.

"Never," said Nikolay.

"So, after you left that shitty motel, we followed the guy. He went up to Mulholland and starting poking around in the bushes, but we grabbed him, bang."

"Bang!" said Nikolay.

"And?" said Farrell.

"*And? And?*" said Nikolay.

"Yeah," said Farrell.

"So, you want us to trust you?" said Nikolay.

"You were talking about business," said Farrell.

"Business isn't all trust," said Pavel.

Pavel and Nikolay looked at each other as they thought it over.

"We're talking to you only to remind you that you should have come to us sooner. You understand what I'm saying?"

"Sure," said Farrell.

"So, we take him to the beach, nice quiet place near Zuma. And I let Pavel talk to him."

Pavel hit his palm with a fist.

"Show me the man, and I'll show you the crime," he said.

"And the crime is this guy was the brother of a movie star. And they were with underage girls," said Nikolay.

"It wasn't easy to get the facts," said Pavel. "How he squealed."

"You know what kind of money that could be worth?" said Nikolay. "So, take this as a warning."

Farrell looked at one and then the other.

"Here's the thing we don't understand. It's like this. We had him on the beach, and we knew about his brother and him, and we were talking over how we could go to the newspapers, and the guy just steps into the water and starts swimming."

"We never saw anything like it," said Pavel.

Each shook his head.

"And why didn't you stop him?" said Farrell.

They shifted their weight from one leg to another, bit a lip, looked around the warehouse. Then Nikolay said, "We don't know how to swim."

"Next time," said Pavel. "Come to see us earlier."

* * *

In Farrell's kitchen, he opened a bottle of wine and poured two glasses, and then Rose Marie came over. He gave her a glass. She sipped her wine, which was the color of sunlight in France.

"That's it," Farrell said. "And I'm changing jobs. Okay?"

She wasn't quite crying, but close, when she sat down next to him.

"I'd like to invite you," he said.

"Where's that?" she said.

"Well, I was thinking about Paris," he said.

"You want me to go with you?" she said.

"Yeah. With me," he said.

"How sweet," she said. "And what would we do?"

"Rent an apartment in Paris," he said. "Go to restaurants. Picnics in the Luxembourg Gardens. Walk along the river."

"What else?" she said.

"Oh," he said. "There's an open-air market off Rue de Buci. Flowers, fruit, vegetables. The guys who sell cheese or pâté will give you a taste if you ask nicely."

She swallowed.

"And after that?"

"Oh, there's a place I know for dinner."

"What's it called?"

"Le Petit Pontoise," he said.

"The kids will be glad. They really will."

"And what about you?" he said.

"Oh, don't be so dumb," she said. "Come on."

"Where are we going?" he said.

"Where do you think?" she said. "We haven't finished our bake-off . . . under that blue skylight. Are you ready?"

"I'll give it my best," he said.

"Good," she said. "You're going to need it."

ABOUT THE AUTHOR

Craig Nova is the author of fourteen novels, which have been translated into ten languages. He has received an Award in Literature from the American Academy and Institute of Arts and Letters, a Guggenheim Fellowship, the Harper-Saxton Prize (previous recipients have been James Baldwin and Sylvia Plath), multiple awards from the National Endowment for the Arts Fellowship, and other prizes. His work has appeared in the *Paris Review, Esquire, New York Times Magazine, Men's Journal,* Best American Short Stories series, and other publications. As a screenwriter he has worked for Touchstone Pictures (a division of the Walt Disney Company), Amblin Entertainment, and other producers. A film was made in 2018 from his novel, *Wetware.*